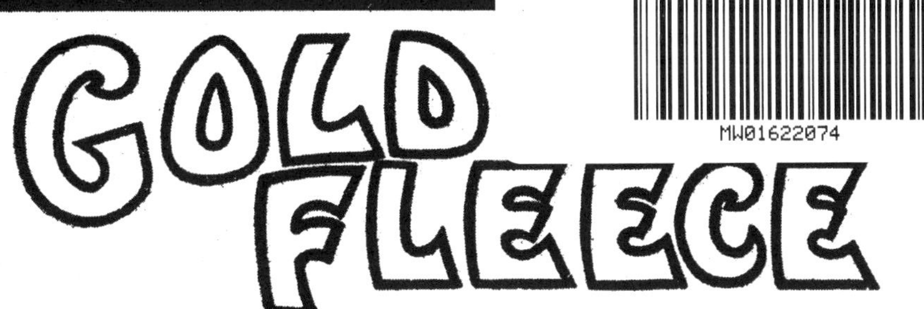

HISTORICAL ADVENTURE MAGAZINE

FEBRUARY 1939 Vol. 2 No. 2

A COMPLETE NOVEL

A NOVELETTE

SHORT STORIES

MISCELLANEOUS

DEPARTMENT

COVER DESIGN

Painted in oils for "Lords of the Tideless Sea" by Harold S. Delay.

These stories are fiction. If any character bears the name of a living person, it is purely a coincidence.

A. J. Gontier, Jr. ASSOCIATE EDITORS C. G. Williams

J. H. Bellamy, Business Manager

Published monthly by Sun Publications. Executive and Editorial Offices, Rand McNally Bldg., 538 So. Clark St., Chicago, Illinois. Copyright 1939 by SUN PUBLICATIONS. Entered as second class matter August 19, 1938, at the Post Office at Chicago, Illinois, under the Act of March 3, 1879. Title Registration applied for at United States Patent Office. Single copy price 20c. Subscriptions in the United States and Canada $2.00 per year. Foreign Postage $1.00 a year extra. Notice to Writers and Artists: When submitting material, please enclose stamped and self-addressed envelope for return if not acceptable. Although care will be exercised in handling unsolicited material, the publishers cannot accept responsibility for its safe return. PRINTED IN U. S. A.

"Eat," ordered Curtogal". Devries looked hard at him. "Eat? Poison perhaps?"

Tideless Sea

by H. BEDFORD-JONES

Illustrated by HAROLD S. DELAY

CHAPTER I

IT WAS on the road from Rome to Naples. Against the roadside hedge of unclipped, wild-sprouting young olive trees, sat the hurt man, watching with proud fierce eyes those who passed. Not many, this morning.

Messer Angelo Bardi, of Florence, was one. He rode down the way with his two servants and his sumpter mules; he dealt only with rich things and great people and was a proud, lusty man, very quick at killing. He saw the hurt man and laughed.

"Ha! The swarthy rogue has fallen foul of bandits!" said he. "Well, I have business in Naples before the *St. Christopher* sails. Ride on! We can do him no good."

Their dust lessened and fell quiet in the sunlight.

The hurt man, who was indeed swarthy, ripped at his already torn garments and made a clumsy bandage for his bleeding thigh. He had numerous wounds, but the thigh was the worst and most painful. He rose and tried to hobble on, toward Naples.

He was well and powerfully built, a soldier to the eye, but dark of skin. The bandage gave way and he sank down again, cursing. He saw another dust, and waited.

Here came the Countess Alix of Forli, with her three laughing demoiselles, and a dozen men-at-arms for guard. They clattered along with the baggage animals trailing, and chattered gaily of Naples and the voyage to Sicily, where the countess, wealthiest woman of Italy, had wide estates.

Lovely was she and lovely were her demoiselles as they talked and laughed; slim rich-gowned bits of fragrance made flesh, agleam with jewels, and the four would have delighted any four men in Christendom, in this happy year of 1516. The captain of the guard would have halted; but one look at the hurt man, and the countess cried out swiftly:

"Halt not! He looks like a rascal; let him be. None of our business if hurt men litter the highway. Besides, he seems to be a Moor, and that were bad luck."

A Moor he was, as his Arabic curses testified. He looked after the gay company, and his fierce eyes were bloodshot with angry threat; but they went their way, and their dust lessened and was gone in the morning sunlight.

PRESENTLY, in the heat of the morning, two sorry hackneys came along the road with one rider. The lead horse gave off a faint banging and clanging, for he bore a load of armor; no very fine armor either, but looked as though it had seen hard service. The rider was bareheaded—a wide, powerful man in faded green travel clothes of English cut. His features were too square and angular for masculine beauty, but strong enough for any need. On his high jackboots were the golden spurs of a knight. The sword, lashed on top of his armor, was a long, straight, heavy beam of steel.

He drew into the roadside, halted his horses, and looked down at the Moor from gray eyes very direct and unafraid.

"Do you need help?" he asked.

"So it seems," said the Moor, half defiantly.

The rider dismounted; once on his feet, he suddenly bulked large, heavy in the arms and shoulders, thin in the waist. His movements were light and deft. From his saddle bags he took leather bottles and other things needful, talking as he did so.

"Assassins?"

"Bandits," said the Moor.

"The same thing. Italy is full of them. I was raised to soldier's work, but never saw as much killing in my life as in the three months I've been here. The time's not been wasted. I've learned a bit of Arabic, and now that the corsairs are swept from the seas and it's safe to travel, I'll go on to Rhodes. Devries is the name, Sir Roger Devries of England."

"I am Mahmud ibn Khalid."

"A Moor, eh?"

"Formerly of Granada, in Spain."

"You don't look that old. It's twenty-four years since the Moors were expelled from Spain, in 1492. You don't look over thirty."

"I'm closer to fifty. You are English, eh?"

"Aye. Going to take service with the Knights of St. John at Rhodes."

"The deadly enemies of the true faith, by Allah?"

"Well, we say the same thing about you Moors of Spain." The gray eyes of Devries twinkled. The two men smiled. "Come, stretch out! That's a bad cut in your thigh, but I have skill with wounds. First, some of this wine?"

Mahmud dissented. "Thanks; my religion forbids."

Devries worked well, washing the

wounds with wine and binding them up. Two ill-assorted men to be found on an Italian highway; but all Italy was ill-assorted in this day. Leo X of Rome fought France and Spain, made peace and fought again, and the world belonged to whom could plunder best and kill fastest.

He looked down at the Moor from gray eyes very direct and unafraid.

Most dreaded name in all Italy of recent times was that of Curtogalli, the Barbary corsair, who had established himself at Bizerta on the African coast. With all the aid of the Turks behind him, Curtogalli raided far and terribly. Not yet had the Black Death come to decimate the world. Italy teemed with humanity, and Curtogalli sent slaves to Stamboul by the thousand. But now, it was said, the Genoese had finished him for ever.

"THERE; now rest a bit, eat some bread and cheese, then I'll mount you behind me," said Devries, and sat down. "You have muscles of iron! What's a Moor doing in Italy?"

Mahmud ibn Khalid smiled. "I was in Rome on business, with a safe-conduct, and last night started for Naples, where I have friends. I was alone, not dreaming of peril. Well, look at me now!" He laughed harshly, fiercely. "A fine plight for a soldier!"

"Bah!" eclaimed Devries. "Fortune

of war, comrade. When I was coming through France, some peasants caught me in a forest. They had me actually hanging to a tree before they discovered I was not a French noble, and then let me go. It's true, I killed a dozen of them," he added with some satisfaction.

The Moor laughed. "At sea, you and I may be enemies; but I think we'd make good friends, comrade. I'm in your debt; I don't forget my debts. Do you need money?"

Devries, munching the cheese, shook his head. "No. I have enough to reach Rhodes. I've already paid passage on the *St. Christopher,* which leaves Naples in a few days, now that the seas are safe for travel and that accursed Curtogalli is dead."

"Eh? Who says he's dead?" demanded the other. Devries shrugged.

"Everyone. The Genoese expedition has destroyed him by this time."

"Allah forbid!"

"Eh?" Devries frowned. "What have you, a soldier and a gentle knight if ever I saw one, in common with that pirate and slaver and arrant rascal?"

The Móor laughed. "He and I both believe in Allah. Our people war on Christians, as Christians war on us. You, for example, go to fight us."

Devries grinned sourly.

"No argument, comrade. Who's this Curtogalli, anyway? Is that his real name?"

"Merely a *nom de guerre;* I understand that his story is similar to my own. Once wealthy, now an exiled wanderer. All due to your fine Christian Spaniards. There were no Barbary Corsairs until we were expelled from Spain and made homeless men."

"So I've heard," admitted Devries, sourly. "And now you make every coast of Europe pay dear!"

"Why not? Wouldn't you do the same, if we took your country and expelled you?"

"Aye. Damn your arguments!" Devries broke into a laugh. "Right or wrong, what matter to me? Facts are facts. I'm a wanderer myself. Fighting your damned corsairs offers me a home, a future, a cause. If men like your Curtogalli didn't make war on women—"

"Ah, there's an argument for that too!" said the Moor, white teeth flashing in a smile. "We send all young women to Stamboul. There they go into harems to breed more men to fight Christians! The Janissaries are all former Christian slaves, or sons of Christian folk. Some of our best fighting stock comes from this source. The two Barbarossa brothers, with the red beards that gave them name . . ."

So the talk went on, a bit merry at the surface, but grave and deadly beneath. Roger Devries liked this Moor, divining in him a fine soldiery man, a splendid comrade had not fate denied. And Mahmud ibn Khalid felt likewise about the Englishman.

"It is a pity we must be foes," he said. "Were this not so, I'd offer you a share in a venture I have afoot, a great and splendid venture, one that will crack the world apart! Christians are in it with me; that was my business in Rome. However, you're not the man to be tempted by wealth and fame to share in anything that would go against your conscience."

Devries gave him a hard, straight look.

"You're right. And you're a man of the same sort; otherwise, you'd not recognize it in me. So you're going to crack the world, are you?"

"Wide open," said the Moor gravely.

"Luck to you, then! You'll do it like a man, if I'm any judge. Shall we go?"

He got the wounded man into the saddle, mounted with him, and set the horses to the road, his armor jingling behind.

To Devries, this Moor was a potential enemy, but he was also a man filled with knightly emprise, with chivalry, with high and powerful character. Cruel, yes; all the world was cruel these days. Who gave mercy, got stabbed in the back.

Life in these lands bordering the tideless sea was very cheap, and death lurked everywhere. At such a game, Roger Devries was the proper man to hold up his own end; his sword-blade, three fingers wide, and his powerful shoulders told this, and most of all his gray eyes and rugged features.

At the gates of Naples they shook hands and separated, the Moor going to an inn close by. And Devries, at least, never expected to see the other man again in this life, except perhaps some day over a sword-edge.

CHAPTER II

NOW Devries had to wait some days before the *St. Christopher* finished her lading and was ready to sail, but he was not alone in this.

She was a stout ship, a *nef* of four masts; the two forward masts were square-rigged, the two after spars carried lateen canvas. Her master, hearty Messer Aldino of Genoa, laughed long and loud when Devries mentioned corsairs. All Naples laughed; indeed, all Italy was laughing with relief, and saying the same thing with zest.

"Three months ago, sir Englishman, Curtogalli carried off five hundred people within twenty miles of Naples itself, and thousands more down the coast. But now, as we speak, what's happening?" Messer Aldino rubbed his horny paws. "That accursed pirate is being destroyed, is no doubt dead now. The whole fleet and army of Genoa are at his lair of Bizerta. The coasts are free, the seas are clear!"

This was truth. The depredations of Curtogalli had passed all bounds. Genoa had poured forth her might, with French assistance. The corsair's base at Bizerta was being wiped out; he and his fleet with it. Italy was safe again. A carrier pigeon had brought home word, brief but sure, that Bizerta was taken.

This fact accounted for the goodly company aboard the *nef*. With Curtogalli raiding there was scant travel of lone ships. Now that all was safe, those who had delayed their voyages took heart to risk the seas. Devries, who had anticipated getting any kind of a ship and poor company, was astonished and delighted by what he found in reality.

The *nef* herself was a big ship, of full nine hundred tons; she carried guns and crew, a couple of hundred soldiers, crossbowmen, bound for Sicily, and many passengers, merchants and others.

Of these, a good score were women, wives and families of officers. Then there was the Countess Alix of Forli, with her three demoiselles, going to her Sicilian estates. Dear God, how beautiful they were! All of them goldenhaired, slim, laughing, richly gowned.

Devries stared his eyes out at them. He had worked up in a hard school of camp and field, and neither knew nor wanted the accomplishments of a lady's man.

Then there was the Florentine merchant, Angelo Bardi, head of the great Bardi trading house with branches everywhere. A man neither young nor old, a lusty arrogant man with shrewd eyes and a nimble tongue whose meaning was never quite certain. He was just from Rome, and knew all the rich and great of the land intimately. Devries did not fancy him; too smooth, too affable, too potentially dangerous. He had heard some queer hints about this man Bardi, during his stay in Italy, and dark hints too.

Still, it was something to be shipmates with such exalted company. Devries sought out the officers and soldiers, who were Genoese mercenaries for the most part, and found them even less to his taste. A ruffling, swaggering lot, more intent on wine and women than any soldiering; also, they disliked Englishmen and said so bluntly. So he left them alone.

ON THE morning the *nef* sailed, Devries was standing by the rail watching the boatmen when the three demoiselles of the countess suddenly surrounded him. Laughing, jesting, they dragged him back to the poopdeck, where Countess Alix sat beneath a sun awning, and presented him. In her white satin gown she looked like an angel, and he was struck dumb by the rare delicate loveliness of her. She laughed merrily, and Messer Bardi, who stood at one side looking on, chuckled to himself.

"What, Sir Englishman!" she exclaimed gaily. "Have they no tongues in your land?"

"Not when beauty strikes them dumb," said he, and felt proud of the fine phrase. But she laughed again, and pointed to the gay silken cushions.

"Come, come, sit down and be at ease! Here's a lute. You shall strum me a madrigal, like a good troubadour."

Devries flushed. "I'm not a troubadour," he blurted. "My only lute is three inches of broad steel. I can play that, but with fine ladies and silken things, I'm awkward."

"You are," she said disdainfully, and dismissed him, with some anger.

None the less, her eyes followed his wide-shouldered figure, and so did the eyes of her merry demoiselles. And so, after a little, did Messer Angelo Bardi, who came up with Devries at the lower rail and stood in talk. He laughed heartily over the incident.

"The countess," he said confidentially, "is a pretty thing, but life has been too kind to her. Her ancestors were fighting men."

"She's all right," said Devries. "I'm no courtier."

"Be glad of it. Courtiers are plenty, honest soldiers few."

With his keen deft face and quick eye and tongue that shrank from nothing, Bardi could be pleasant when he so desired. He was a friend of princes, too. Leo X, who ruled in Rome, was a Medici, son of Lorenzo the Magnificent of Florence; Bardi knew him well. Devries perforce was courteous, and when they fell into talk of corsairs, as all travelers must who dared the sea, he broached the argument put forward by Mahmud ibn Khalid—though he said nothing of his meeting with the Moor.

"I'm not a troubadour," he blurted, "My only lute is three inches of broad steel."

Bardi listened and nodded thoughtfully.

"It rings true, Sir Englishman. Many Spanish Moors were very gentle knights and learned men and wise scholars; they were swept out into exile ruthlessly. They took to the seas, since Barbary offered their closest refuge, and vengeance. I've met more than one of them—bitter, cruel men, though they've harmed me not."

"They've pillaged your goods, at least?"

Bardi laughed. "No. If this ship were taken tomorrow by Barbarossa or Curtogalli, I'd be quite safe."

"I'd like to know why," grunted Devries, who did not like the man by half.

"Because I have a safe-conduct from the Sultan himself, like many a good trader these days. And it is respected by the corsairs, with reason. A fifth of all their booty, and most of their slaves, go to Stamboul. So I'm safe enough."

"Hm! I prefer this safe-conduct," and Devries touched the sword he was wearing now. He nodded toward the Genoese crossbowmen down the deck. "Or those."

"Every man to his own taste," said Messer Angelo Bardi, smiling. "Perhaps you're right. Now that Curtogalli is rooted out and destroyed, Rome is safe."

"Rome, safe?" echoed Devries, astonished. "Rome, mistress of Italy, was never in danger from those rascally pirates."

"Little you know." Bardi leaned on the rail, spoke softly. "Why, Rome's a hotbed of intrigue and plots. Leo is a fat pleasure-seeker, no soldier. Still, she's center of the whole Christian world; haven't you heard the ugly rumors?"

Devries shrugged, and glanced across the water at Naples and the lessening hills. The *nef* was on her way at last, men tramping the deck, canvas filling to the breeze, the sea ahead.

"Rumors? They're nothing to me," he said curtly.

"Facts would be. To you and the whole world. The Crusaders took Jerusalem; what if the Turks took Rome and destroyed her, as the Vandals did a thousand years ago?"

"Are you serious?" Devries frowned at the Florentine.

"Quite. Such a project was actually on foot recently; and, I heard, it was engineered from within Rome itself, by certain great men who hate the Medici pope. Curtogalli was the man to do it, sailing up the Tiber and planting the Crescent over the ruins of the Vatican. That's why the expedition against him was pushed. Now he's dead or sent in flight to Stamboul, and the danger's gone. But it did exist."

"I don't believe it," Devries said bluntly. "No honest men would betray their own city and people to infidel pirates."

Bardi chuckled and fingered his smooth, strong chin.

"My good knight, when men become rich and great, they cease to be honest."

"Not the right kind of men," said Devries. He put meaning into the words, put all his dislike of the man into them; and Bardi, flushing slightly, went his way.

ROGER DEVRIES scowled after him. Rumors, eh? Plots, hatched within the dissolute circles of Rome itself—ah, it was good to be at sea and away from Italy! He disliked Italians. Assassination and treachery were too common here for his taste.

He looked aft at the Countess Alix and her three pretty demoiselles, and sought an empty corner of the deck, to sit and eat his own coarse provender. Noon was past, and the *nef* bowling along on an even keel, standing down the coast.

Devries longed for the day, soon to come now, when he would be aboard a war-galley, with work to do and blows to give. His armor was below in his cabin. He had learned Arabic—at least, had learned to speak it fairly—as part of his preparations; he was eager for the life ahead. The knights of Rhodes maintained warfare, day and night, year in and year out, in protection of Christian ships.

It did not occur to Roger Devries that many a person aboard the big *nef* might find in this voyage a ploy of destiny that would alter lives and characters and all the future, and wipe them out of the world.

The afternoon was half over when the three little sails were sighted. They stood in between the *nef* and the coastline. Genoese galleys heading north, said Messer Aldino the ship-master; perhaps bearing fuller news of the destruction of Bizerta and the corsair Curtogalli.

They were, most certainly, galleys, with oars aflash in the sun, making the standard galley-pace of three knots an hour. There was no sea running, and the rails of the *nef* were crowded with watchers as the three galleys drew closer. Sharply, a seaman sent down a shout from aloft.

"Corsairs, master! They answer no signals, and they have cannon!"

Consternation and amazement swept the decks. Corsairs, infidels? Impossible! The seas were swept clean of corsairs. Yet the laughing women fell silent and anxious. Messer Aldino reassured everyone that it was impossible, that alarm was needless. Genoese galleys carried cannon.

None the less, the ship-master fell desperately to work. He whistled up all the crew, broke out gunpowder, loaded the cannon, and served out arms. A trumpet blew, and the crossbowmen formed up amidships.

Devries eyed the three galleys, now a scant quarter-mile distant. He eyed the Genoese officers, the alarm sweeping the decks into panic. He saw that the galleys were now sweeping around a trifle, and spreading out. Grimly, he went below, got out his armor, and buckled it on. He had just finished, when an outbreak of shrieks and hoarse cries brought him up to the deck in haste, and he saw the reason. The leading galley was suddenly black with armed men, had run up the green flag of Islam, and her oars were spurting. All three were circling to come at the *nef*. A gun spoke, and another.

They were long, low craft, quite narrow; that the stout *nef* should fear them, standing high above them as she did, seemed fantastic. But it was a fantastic moment. Devries watched with a curious sense of unreality. Time stood still; upon him rushed an overpowering visual acuity—a sharp and awful clearness of mental vision, a momentary flash of terrible perception.

Corsairs, yes; the yell of "Allah!" was enough. Men fanatic, who lived to fight, who fought with reckless courage and welcomed death; and here, down these decks, hurried panic, inefficient action, craven hearts that thought only of safety. In this flash of perception, he knew what the end must be.

Then everything changed, reality swept back, and he was himself. The leading galley blossomed with white smoke, and her guns roared. Down the decks swept death, wild shrieks, men rolling and blood spurting. Devries went to the officers of the Genoese.

"Can you use me?" he said.

"Good God, messer knight!" burst out one. "Take command!"

"Very well." Devries wasted no words. "Post your men along the bulwarks to take cover. Hold fire until I give the word. Let Messer Aldino work his guns. Cover! The bowmen in two ranks."

HE HAD never fought at sea, but his calm demeanor heartened them; they obeyed. He stood beside the tiller. Arrows were flying in air, striking all around. A din of yells came from the galleys as they closed in, with roll of drums and trumpets all ablare. "Allah! Allah!" lifted the shrill uproar of voices, as the three low ships swung and swept in upon their prey.

Guns belched. The pierieres of all three galleys let go—wide-mouthed guns, belching fifty pounds of broken stone to a charge. Grapnels were flung, caught, held.

"Fire!" ordered Devries, staggering a trifle from shock as an arrow shattered on his breast-plate.

Along the bulwarks, the Genoese uprose. Crossbows twanged and twanged again; the bolts hurtled into the crowded masses of men below. The yells became screams and shrieks. But the galleys clung there like leeches. Men chopping at the grapnel-lines were picked off. The Genoese paused to wind up their crossbows; brown faces, helmets, axes, uprose along the bulwarks. Messer Aldino was down with an arrow through his eye, and panic seized the shipmen. They broke, abandoned their guns, disorganized the Genoese. More and more brown faces came clambering up. The yells of "Allah" were on the deck, now.

Devries, in sudden ghastly dismay, realized that his first meeting with the corsairs of Islam was turning out badly. And he could do nothing about it.

Now it was hand to hand, clumps of Saracens on the deck, swords out. Devries bared his sword, swung the heavy blade, and strode down into the midst of it. The heavy steel clashed and clanged. They broke before him. Weapons struck him and glanced. Brown fierce faces, white faces of renegades, went reeling in red ruin from him.

He knew he was fighting, however; these men gave him grim work. Now uprose a mailed foe, an Arab or Moorish knight, heavily armed. Weapons clanged anew, the Moor, with the thirsty sword half through his body, fell away. Devries strode on. An Arab, fierce and eager, leaped out before him. Men gave back. Here was a corsair of note, obviously. His curved scimitar struck and slashed, but the big sword met it squarely; Devries pushed up, breast to breast, struck suddenly with the sword-pommel, and as the Arab staggered, cut sideways. That man died, and others rushed in.

Of a sudden, Devries realized the unwelcome truth that he was alone. Panic had seized the Genoese, as fresh corsairs came tumbling over the rail. They broke before the wave of desperate fighting men, they lost heart, they fled.

Devries, warring on, found himself ringed in. He backed against the rail and fought on stubbornly. He was unwounded, though many a weapon had given him bruises through the good metal. Then a stone struck his helm and dizzied him. His sword wavered and fell; an Arab leaped for his throat. He killed that man, but the weight unsteadied him. He lost balance, his foot slipped with blood on the deck.

He was down. With a terrific crash, a mace struck his helm; it stunned him, left him unconscious for a minute or two. No more, but enough.

He wakened; now he was alone among the dead and hurt; with an aching head, securely lashed hand and foot. His whirling brain cleared. The fight had swept away. It had all lasted scarcely ten minutes; purpose and efficiency winning quickly over half-hearted measures.

As he sat, propped against the bulwark, he stared dully along the deck. It was thick, now, with men of all races —renegades, Arabs, blacks, Turks, Moors. The crew and the Genoese were being slaughtered to a man. "Allah!" lifted triumphant yells. "Allah! Curtogalli! Curtogalli!"

Devries groaned and closed his eyes. Curtogalli was dead, destroyed—yet these corsairs must be his men! It was past understanding. He drooped wearily, mind and body.

SILENCE, comparative silence, ensued; then a burst of voices close at hand. He looked up. A warrior in Persian chain-mail, a renegade with red hair and blue eyes, was directing a number of men. The killing had ceased, the bodies were being tossed over the rail.

"Leave that one with the golden spurs!" cried the renegade. "A knight. He is mine, for ransom. Hurt him not!"

"Aye, Rais Hassan," came the chorus. Rais—that meant captain, thought Devries dully. Captain of one of the galleys, no doubt. They swept away from him. Dead and dying were tossed over, Moslem and Christian alike. Those who could care for their own wounds, escaped.

Some came and stared at Devries, but not many. Attention was soon diverted, as the prisoners came pouring up from below—women, infants, passengers, fugitives. Devries, well up on the higher poop deck, had hideous view of everything. Most of the men were killed at once. A few of the younger were stripped and sent down to the galleys, to replace slaves who had died at the oars. Screams resounded; they were drowned by bursts of laughter from the corsairs, whose jests flew fast.

Devries jerked up his head, as Messer Bardi appeared. Rais Hassan and two other commanders, examining each who came, heard his rapid speech, listened to him, examined his papers. He was released.

"By Allah, you are lucky!" said Rais Hassan, grinning. "Go down to my ship as a guest; Curtogalli will welcome you."

"Curtogalli!" exclaimed Bardi, who spoke Arabic fluently. "But he is dead!"

A roar of laughter greeted this.

"Not yet," said Rais Hassan. "We gave Bizerta to the Genoese, and came

He lost balance, his foot slipped on the deck.

north to make a fair exchange. Off with you!"

The Florentine, somewhat shaken by this information, went his way.

Curtogalli, eh? Devries wondered. The corsair was said to have a score of galleys, six or seven thousand men at least. Giving up Bizerta to the Genoese, sailing north to strike at the undefended Italian coasts—

Then Devries groaned a little and forgot everything else, as Countess Alix and her demoiselles, no longer laughing, came on deck. She was separated from the three, and brought before Rais Hassan and the two other captains. What she said, Devries could not hear; but she was cold, disdainful, arrogant. Then the voice of Rais Hassan lifted.

"You need to learn your lesson. A Christian is less than a dog; you have no more value than your worth in the slave-market."

He struck her across the face, then put out his hand and tore the white robe from her. She stood among them all, unclad, shrinking, alone. Rais Hassan ripped at her robe, dabbled it in a pool of blood on the deck, and flung the fragments at her.

"There, woman; take it. Soon you'll feel the whips on your white skin—ha! In the name of Allah, what's this?"

Sudden diversion broke in, laughter, screams, shrieks. The three demoiselles had been seized and snatched away. Rais Hassan, in towering fury, had them led up, and the men who had taken them.

"They are for Curtogalli to give, not for you to take!" he said to the men, and motioned his warriors. "Kill them!"

Those men were cut down on the spot. The four young women were taken down to the galley of Rais Hassan. The latter beckoned one of the other captains.

"Take what men you must have, and sail this *nef* to Stamboul. Your galley with her; stop near Messina and fill her with slaves. These other women? Bah! They're not worth taking to market. Let them be shared among your men."

He came down the deck to Devries, and halted, speaking in the lingua franca that was understood everywhere along the tideless sea.

"Ha, sir knight! You go to Curtogalli with us. Your fate is in his hands. Will you give your knightly parole until we reach him, tonight or tomorrow?"

"Yes," said Devries.

He was put on his feet, freed, stripped of his armor, and sent down a ladder of rope to the galley alongside. As he went, the clamorous laughter of the corsairs dinned up to the sunset sky, and the shrieks of what women remained aboard there.

And thus, for Roger Devries, the old life ended and a new began; and not for him alone. The prelude to adventure was done.

CHAPTER III

DARKNESS, and sobbing women. The laughter of the demoiselles was done.

With the four of them, Devries was shoved into a tiny cabin aboard the galley, given a bowl of food, and left to merciful obscurity. For a while silence reigned. The galley tossed abominably. From the oar-benches in the waist came the steady creak and groan of oars and men, the undeviating, monotonous pound of the drum that set

He tore the white robe from her.

the time, occasionally the crack of a whip and a screaming cry.

"Still silent, Sir Englishman?"

Devries turned to the soft, huddled figure beside him. Her hands fluttered at his hurt head; to his astonishment, he found her washing off the blood and bandaging the split scalp with a fragment of her tattered gown. His heart warmed toward her. She, at least, was not sobbing like the others. Her ancestors had been fighting men.

"Sweet lady, what words would avail us?"

"None. You are right," she replied. "We are going into hell. Not you, perhaps."

"Comfort." He seized her little hand and pressed it. "I give you thanks. If I might, I'd offer you devotion and service."

She laughed bitterly. "What you refused this morning, you'd give now?"

"When you most need it, sweet lady," said he, and his soul swelled within him for aching love of her. "When hope is least. Aye!"

"You're a strange man," she replied, a break in her voice. "What do you lose? Home and family, friends, rank, position?"

"I've little to lose," he said frankly. "I've earned my spurs among fighting men. Behind me is nothing. Since I was fifteen, I've been with armies. I'm no courtier."

"So you told me this morning." Her fingers fluttered on his face like a benison. "What service can you give me now? I am lost, less than nothing, a chattel. Ah, God! That one day should bring such changes! Perhaps it's punishment for my pride."

"I give what I can," he returned. She sighed.

"Good. I accept, then, in humility. If you had a dagger—"

"For yourself? No, no!"

"For that fiend in human form, Curtogalli!" she broke in with a catch of breath.

"No," he said again. "Wait. There may come a time, a chance. See, sweet lady, I give you my whole devotion and service from this day forth! Wait, and trust."

"You talk like a monk," she answered bitterly. "Trust! Whom?"

"Me," he rejoined. "And God."

She made a little scornful, inarticulate sound, and said nothing more. But Devries, when he sank into the slumber of utter weariness, still clung to her slender hand.

Once, toward morning, he was wakened by yells. The cabin had one tiny window, less for air than for sight, and he rose to it. The oars were stilled, motion had ceased. Looking forth, as the galley swung he caught lights near at hand. At first he thought they were in some harbor. Then he saw the lights were bobbing, not fixed. A voice from a number of seamen at the rail reached him.

"Only twenty fathom, they say; make the anchor good and fast. Allah is with us! Ten miles at sea, and only twenty fathom! Just let the weather hold fine and—"

The voice died, the men moved away. Devries sank down again.

Ten miles at sea! Since the *nef* was taken, the galley had continued north. She must, then, be a bit beyond Naples; not in any port, but ten miles at sea. Those lights? Other galleys. Probably a score in all. Anchored off the Italian coast, then; the whole fleet of the corsair Curtogalli. Why?

Apprehension gathered in Devries; the words of that Moor on the highway came back to his mind—a venture that would crack the world apart! What, then? Had it something to do with Curtogalli? Perhaps. That wily corsair had let the Genoese fleet and army go to Bizerta, capture his base, do what they like; he, meantime, had doubled back up the coast of Italy with his sea-wolves. Why?

Messer Angelo Bardi, somewhere aboard here, and his rumors about Rome captured and destroyed. Ah, nonsense, nonsense! Such things could not happen in the world. It was all wild gossip. Curtogalli was here, however, doubtless to raid and get away again.

"And I'm here," said Devries to himself, unhappily, as he fell asleep.

WITH morning, came food and action. Ordered on deck, Devries found two other craft bearing down, and fenders being put out. The sea was like a millpond, smooth as glass, with scarcely a swell; Curtogalli and another were coming aboard. He did not need the talk of those around to know that the splendid galley bearing down to larboard was that of Curtogalli. The craft spoke for herself. Painted all pure white, with oarblades gilded and brass cannon aglitter, she looked more like the pleasure craft of some princely seaman than a pirate galley. An awning of brilliant hues shaded her after-deck.

No less curious was the second craft, coming in on the starboard side. A galeasse, this, a larger craft using both sails and oars, with the rowing benches decked over and high forecastle and sterncastle at either end bearing heavy guns. The flag of Venice blew at her stern; instead of the galley's enormous lateen sail, she carried three masts and with her higher sides was a veritable fortress. Obviously a prize, for the Lion of Venice was everywhere aboard her—flag, bulwarks, stern, high prow—and her three slanting sails were worked with the Lion and the Cross.

Rais Hassan came down the deck, saw Devries, and approached him with a grin.

"Talk ransom to Curtogalli, sir knight, and talk your best!"

"I have nothing," said Devries. "There's none to pay ransom for me."

The renegade drew down his shaggy red brows in a scowl.

"If that be true, by Allah! you get chained to a rower's bench!"

"Perhaps," said Devries. He was minded to fight and make them kill him, rather than accept fate meekly. But he had given his parole until he faced Curtogalli. A smile grew in his eyes as he faced the renegade. "Was it you who struck me down yesterday?"

"Aye." Rais Hassan surveyed him. "Why do you ask?"

"To know where the debt lies."

The other laughed. "So? You're a slave now, not a soldier. And before you're chained to the rowing bench, I'll give you a hundred lashes to break your spirit."

"That time has not yet come," said Devries. "What will happen to the Countess Alix?"

"Oh, the haughty wench? She'll go to the Sultan as a gift."

"Foolish waste of good money, Rais Hassan. Send him another."

"Eh? What mean you?"

"She's said to be wealthy. Ask Messer Bardi. You might ransom her at high price."

Rais Hassan whistled. "Ha! Say you so? It's worth a thought; but Curtogalli may say otherwise." The renegade's face darkened, and a French oath came to his lips. "That dog-brother needs a lesson or two himself, and may get one yet. Well, I'll lighten your chains by way of gratitude for the idea."

He went hurrying away with a blare of orders, as the two other craft swept in alongside and lines were flung, to make them fast.

Devries felt a little prickling up his spine—a thrill of hope, of comprehension. This Rais Hassan had been a Frenchman, then, before he turned Turk. And he did not love Curtogalli; hated the commander, in fact, if his face were any criterion. For all his cool imperturbable mask, Roger Devries had set his brain at work, and he had one. He was dealing with men now, with soldiers, and meant to catch at any straw that offered.

There was the Florentine now—Messer Bardi, stopping for a word with Rais Hassan, coming on aft to the rail where Devries stood. He was smiling, composed, shrewd.

"Ha! Good morning to you, Englishman. You fought well yesterday, I hear."

"Did you?" came the blunt question.

"Fighting's not my job, sir knight," Bardi rejoined affably. "Let me advise you to make friends with this Rais Hassan. He's a far more capable man than Curtogalli, I hear."

"He seems to think so," said Devries. The other chuckled enjoyably.

"Aye, true! It's nothing to me; I'm in no danger. But I'd hate to see you chained to an oar for life."

"In that case, you might pay my ransom and save me from it," Devries said with some irony. Bardi looked down his nose.

"Ha! I fear that's impossible. But," he added, lowering his voice, "you and I might yet turn a deal with Rais Hassan. Would you be willing?"

"I'd be willing for anything with honor," said Devries.

"Admirable! Curtogalli has played a shrewd trick on the Genoese; now he means to raid the unsuspecting coast, and get away. There's a price of fifty thousand golden ducats on his head. A share of that, and freedom—eh? Mind you, it's no easy task. They say he's a superb swordsman—"

DEVRIES scarcely heard the smooth voice. The words did not reach him. He was suddenly absorbed in what he saw under the awning of the galley alongside. He caught at the Florentine's arm.

"Aye, of course, I'm willing! But look—isn't that Curtogalli himself? It could be no other. And fully armed!"

"They say he's never unarmed while at sea. Aye. That must be our man."

That awning, that after-deck, was close beside them; every detail stood clear, and the details were gorgeous. Over the deck was spread a superb Turkish rug. A number of black slaves stood about, bearing dishes and trays. The corsair, obviously, was sharing the morning meal with his lucky captains. Several of these surrounded him, some armed, some not, in a blaze of jewels and weapons. All a setting, it seemed, for the central figure.

Seated cross-legged was Curtogalli. Little could be seen of his swarthy features; like Rais Hassan, he affected a Persian helmet with long nose-piece and dangling chain mail that fell about cheeks and neck; but his helmet was studded with jewels. His body was covered with a long chain-coat, heavily gilded; across his knees was a long scimitar, the curved blade naked, the hilt a mass of coruscating gems.

"They're coming for you!" exclaimed Messer Bardi abruptly. "Leave all to me, and anger them not. We may yet have luck—"

He hurried away. Between the two galleys had been placed a gangway over the rails amidships. Two men were coming, intent upon Devries, ordering him along; others were smashing into the cabin to get the Countess Alix. Devries followed without protest, and found himself aboard the white galley. He was led aft, into the crowd about the corsair chief.

Rais Hassan and the other captain stood in talk before Curtogalli, as before some king. And the voices that rose were tense with anger.

"So you sent Rais Ham'illah away with the *nef* you captured!" said Curtogalli. Devries could just follow the Arabic words. "Why, you fool, you fool!"

"By Allah! Not even you can call me fool!" cried Rais Hassan furiously.

"Let me prove it." Curtogalli laughed, and the laugh was harsh. "We need every ship we can get, for slaves and booty here. Your orders were to bring in any ships you found. You get a big one, and send it to Stamboul! Send it to pick up a few hundred women and children down the coast—when it should have been filled with treasure, with all the treasure of Rome, with children of the greatest Christian families!"

"Rome?" faltered Rais Hassan in obvious amazement.

"Aye." The voice of Curtogalli became metallic, staccato with anger. "Rome! I tell you now, I tell all of you, what our errand is here. We plunder Rome itself! Within four days, the loot of Rome will be ours!"

There was a moment of stupefied silence. Then a bursting yell arose—a yell so fierce, so exultant, so wildly frenzied as it spread along the decks, that the amazed Devries could not repress a shiver. These wolves, let loose on the imperial city!

"But—but—that is impossible!" exclaimed Rais Hassan. "We have a scant six or seven thousand men in all. Rome is not on the sea. It has strong walls—"

The voice of Curtogalli silenced him in scathing accents.

"We have swords, Rais Hassan, and a leader! And I'm the leader. I've made all arrangements. The city will be ours at the first assault—even without an assault, if all goes well. Rome—ours without a battle! You need not understand. I'm not telling my plans yet. Well, after all you've made a good capture; Allah bless you! Now let us see these women."

COUNTESS ALIX was led forward. Her three demoiselles were kept a little back. Curtogalli eyed her intently, and Rais Hassan spoke to him quickly, eagerly. The chieftain shook his head.

"No. I will not ransom her. She shall be a gift to the Padishah, the Sultan Soliman. A woman of rank—good! She will please him. Ransom? Bah! All the wealth of Rome shall be yours to pick from, Hassan. Keep her aboard your own ship; you shall be responsible for her safety and well-being—to the Sultan himself, mind! If you fail, you'll be put on a stake in the Stamboul market. Send her away."

The Countess Alix, understanding nothing of what was said, was led away by two men. She caught the eye of Devries, and he made a gesture of reassurance, as she disappeared.

"These other three?" Curtogalli looked at the demoiselles. "Let them serve her? No. We've no use for servants, when every ship will be crowded with slaves from the greatest of Roman families! Give these to any who wants them. Who'll have them?"

"I," spoke out Hassan quickly. "One of them—the little one."

"Take her, then." Curtogalli sank back, laughing. "Who next?"

A clamor uprose. Hassan strode to the demoiselles and picked up the youngest in his two hands, grinning widely; two other men seized upon the remaining pair, and their shrieks died quickly away.

"Now," said Curtogalli, "bring up the others—who? Oh, yes. The Florentine. And the Englishman who fought so hard. Where are they?"

A knife pricked Devries forward. Messer Bardi joined him. They stood before the corsair, at the edge of the carpet. Curtogalli was eating some fruit from a tray that one of the blacks handed him, and broke off to stare at the two men. Then he leaned back, laughing heartily to himself, and beckoned.

"Florentine! Come hither," he said in Italian. Something in the words, in the accent, in the voice, plucked vaguely at the memory of Devries, as Messer Bardi took a step or two forward. "So you have a safe-conduct from Stamboul itself, eh?"

"Yes. Here it is, Rais," and Bardi produced a scroll.

"Good. You are safe; but you must go to Stamboul with me."

"What?" Bardi turned livid. "To Stamboul? Why is that?"

"To answer charges against you. A week ago, as you rode to Naples, you passed a hurt man on the highway. Did you help him? No. Instead, you told your servants to ride on, that you had business in Naples. But that wounded man, Messer Bardi, was one of the Enlightened, one of the Faithful, a True Believer. A Moor. And because you did not help him—"

Bardi broke into frenzied protests. Curtogalli munched his fruit and laughed. Those around laughed. At a word and a look from the chieftain, one of the black slaves came to Devries, and presented it to the astonished Englishman. It held bread and salt.

"Eat!" ordered Curtogalli. Devries looked hard at him.

"Eat? Poison, perhaps?"

"No, bread and salt of hospitality." Curtogalli reached up and removed the jeweled Persian helmet, and laid it aside. He smiled at Devries. "I shall pay your ransom, my friend; you are as my brother. Eat! It is the law of Islam, if you eat my bread and salt you are under my protection—"

Dazed, uncertain, stupefied with the recognition, Devries obeyed and ate. It had taken him all this while to realize that Curtogalli was the Moor he had helped on the highway, Mahmud ibn Khalid of the wounds.

CHAPTER IV

"MY FRIEND, you shall be set free, unharmed, with the finest weapons and garments and a rich purse," said Curtogalli. "But not now."

"I don't want your garments and money; the weapons, I'll take," said Devries sturdily. "But what about Countess Alix?"

"Don't mention her again. She goes to Stamboul."

"Let her free, ransom her; take me instead."

At these words, Curtogalli turned grave, astonished, probing eyes on the speaker.

The morning was wearing on; the three ships still clung together, the rest of the fleet remained anchored around. Curtogalli and Devries sat alone beneath the awning.

"Are you serious? You can't be such a fool! Chivalry of that sort is folly," said the Moor. Devries shrugged.

"I mean it. I am devoted to the service of that lady, while I live."

"So?" The other smiled, his white teeth flashing. "Well, in that case I may reverse myself. We'll see. There are greater women in Rome who'll please the Sultan."

Devries laughed a little. "Now I'm the one to ask if you're serious."

"Yes, as Allah lives!" The swift fanatic light in the dark eyes leaped high. "The plans are made. That's why I was in Rome—I, Curtogalli! What did I tell you? A venture that would crack the world wide open? This is it."

"You must be mad to think of it," said Devries sternly. "Not sixty thousand men could conquer Rome!"

"Six thousand fighting men are worth sixty thousand cravens. Mine fight." The corsair was all aflame now. "Mad? Not a bit of it, my friend. Today, this very day, the pope leaves Rome and goes to his seashore villa at Padiglione. This afternoon, I go there in the galeasse of Venice, openly; she will arouse no suspicion at all. Many ships put in there for water.

"Tonight we land and seize Leo of Rome. The galleys come in, we push up the Tiber, straight for Rome itself. Even if my friends there fail to deliver the city, we hold the pope. We trade him for Rome; at worst, we assault. Blood and fire! Before any force can gather, we're gone, and Rome is sacked."

Devries, listening with a soldier's ear, felt a cold chill grip at him. Here, he perceived, was no boast at all, but careful planning. He knew that Leo X spent much of the summer at the seashore, and this fact made the wild dream certain to succeed. If Curtogalli held the pope captive, Rome was his; the city would be in blind, mad panic. And not all Rome could muster a thousand men to fight with the reckless deviltry of these corsairs—to fight as fought the damned.

"Aye," he said slowly, grudgingly. "You'll win. Seize the pope, and you must win. But you were wounded! How can you act as you must?"

The Moor shrugged. "The wound's healing; I can get about. A soldier, as you should know, isn't stopped by mere wounds. Only by death. But now I must leave you until later. All the captains are coming aboard for a meeting with me, and discussion of plans and orders."

He rose, and went on quickly, smiling:

"You're free to do what you wish, go where you like. See the Countess Alix, if that pleases you. No one will offer you harm, for you're known to be my guest now. And if you choose to accompany us ashore tonight and then go free, you have but to say the word. We'll see, later."

So saying, he strode away, giving no indication of his recent wounds. Devries looked after him, eyeing the fine soldierly figure with lowering gaze; a corsair and pirate the man might be, a follower of Mahound, a hater of all Christian things, but he had a touch of fine chivalry, of generous warmth, none the less.

"If he were anything but what he is, I'd love him!" thought Devries. "But as it is—ah! I have no choice."

None, indeed. Curtogalli himself had voiced words that now lingered in his mind with terrible echoes. This man could be stopped by only one thing: Death.

MATCHING the Moor's generosity with his own, Devries had been tempted to utter impulsive warning about possible plots, having in his heart the words of Messer Bardi. Now he was glad he had not. For, with gloomy but stern conviction, he saw that nothing but some such chance stood between Curtogalli and a reeling Christendom struck to the heart by a vital blow.

He sat there watching the boats come in from the other galleys. He saw the captains come aboard. Rais Hassan, the French renegade, and the master of the Venetian galeasse came over the rail from either side, and trooped below with the rest, to the meeting that would decide the fate of half the world.

For, to Roger Devries, destiny showed clear portents. Dissolute, treacherous, weak, Rome might be; but to the whole world she was a symbol of greater things. Leo X might be a sorry ruler, a plump white-fingered pleasure lover, but he was pope. Let Rome lie in stricken ashes, and the whole Moslem world would be fired to fresh conquest, to new wars. The pope a captive, Rome sacked—aye, Christendom might well reel! And these things, incredible as they were, fantastic and unthinkable as they were, would happen within three days.

An officer, a lean brown Arab, came up to Devries with a smile.

"Lord, our master gave orders that you might select what weapons pleased you from those in the armory."

"Later, thanks." Devries came to his feet. "Have you any wine?"

"None, lord. It is forbidden by our faith."

"Then send me a slave with some food and water, to take to the woman aboard Rais Hassan's galley. I have permission to visit her."

The Arab assented readily, and a black arrived to follow Devries. The Englishman was only dimly aware of the tremendous change in his own fortunes; he was no longer a Christian dog, he was now a friend and guest of Curtogalli.

He paid scant heed, however, to the smiles that met him, the eager words of greeting, the courtesy on all sides. He was troubled by his own problems, and groaned within himself as he crossed to the galley of Rais Hassan.

There, he was taken to the cabins without demur. As he gained them, two slaves passed him, carrying between them a slim stark thing draped in golden hair. It was the young demoiselle who had been given to Rais Hassan, and there was a dagger buried to the haft in her bosom. The two others, perhaps, had encountered a less easy release.

He encountered Messer Angelo Bardi, who came eagerly to speak with him, but Devries would not.

"Later," he said, putting aside the Florentine. "First I must have word with the Countess Alix."

So he came to her. The black left his food and drink; the countess, her cheeks streaked by the mark of tears, stared at him hard.

"What is it?" she gasped. "What is it? You've changed—"

"I've brought you something to eat, sweet lady," said Devries, and sank down on the edge of the bunk. He passed a hand over his eyes. "I need help. I know not where honor stands. I—God forgive me, I don't know what's right! This Curtogalli is my friend. I saved his life, not knowing who he was. Now he's set me free, and I think he will listen to my plea for you."

"Then we should rejoice!" she exclaimed, with sudden hope and joy breaking in her eyes. "If this is true, we should be glad—but you're not glad!"

"No, I am not," said Devries. "You don't know what's about to happen."

He told her, bluntly, all Curtogalli proposed to do.

In her face, as though in the face of the world itself, he saw mirrored the mixed emotions that would sweep over the earth at this news. Incredulity, horror, an appalled fear; not for herself, but for the destruction of the city that had been a symbol and a power for a thousand years redoubled.

"Rome!" she said, choking. "If Rome is taken, then the Turks will pour into Italy from every side—"

"Not into Italy alone," he broke in grimly. "It means they'll sweep over the whole of Christendom with an impetus nothing can resist. It means heartbreak and lost hope and weakness to all of Europe. It means a flood of fleets and corsairs raiding every coast in all Christian countries. And I could —I might—stop it."

"You!" she gasped, wide-eyed. "You! How?"

"I don't know yet. To me this man is courteous, friendly, unsuspicious; he would never dream that I would plot against him. Where lies honor?" Devries groaned a little in his mental anguish, and gazed at her from bloodshot eyes.

Gradually she comprehended what tore at him. And when she did understand, she smiled softly, tenderly, and took his hand, and uttered words that he would never have expected from her a day earlier.

"Dear gentle knight, what do little folks like us matter, after all? He is your friend, you say; what does he matter, either? Or your honor? You have to think of but one thing. Not ourselves, not Rome, not the faith in which we were bred; only of the awful untold suffering that will come upon the world, our world, if this man accomplishes his intent. Your country is far away, but it, too, will suffer."

"Ah!" Devries lifted his head. "But I swore to you my knightly devotion; my heart seconds it, sweet lady. You are more to me than all the earth—"

A smile struggled again to her lips, though terror lay in her eyes.

"Don't think of me; I release you from your offer. Your honor lies far beyond all that. If I could help you, I would. I'll prove it if the chance arises. But think only of the one important thing, the one great thing, true knight!"

Roger Devries was in many ways a

very simple fellow, seeing right or wrong as straight roads, with no curves. He was not used to arguing himself into any way that pleased him, with fine phrases and smooth words. In the words of this girl, however, he found a quiet earnestness that set his heart at rest.

He kissed her slim fingers, and, reassured and once more steady in his heart, went forth to find Messer Angelo Bardi, who was awaiting him anxiously.

CHAPTER V

IT WAS high noon, and food was being served out.

Bardi, who had made quite the best of his own situation, led the Englishman into his own cabin, food was brought, and the two of them were left alone. Devries, unhurried, ate heartily and quickly.

"Well?" said the Florentine. "You know everything—the rumors were true. Where do you stand?"

"With you," said Devries. "There's no middle ground, Messer Bardi. What hope from Rais Hassan?"

"Ah!" Bardi caught his breath and spoke softly. "Every hope. Hassan wants to lead this raid on Rome himself. He's been cheated at every turn. Curtogalli derided him and scorned him in public, before all the captains, for sending away the *nef*. The girl given him stabbed herself, before he could have his will of her. He's furious, boiling inwardly, ready for anything!"

Devries smiled.

"So? There's not much time to waste. Do you know the plan? The Venetian ship puts into shore this night. The pope is to be seized at his villa."

"I know," said the Florentine, his features working curiously. He, too, was somehow stricken by the thought of it all. "But remember, fifty thousand gold ducats is a lot of money to anyone! Even to Rais Hassan. If I give him a bill of exchange on my Stamboul branch for that amount, the thing is settled. It depends on you. Yes or no?"

"Yes," said Devries promptly.

The other drew a quick, sharp breath of relief.

"Ah! I was in doubt. I had heard that Curtogalli welcomed you as a friend and brother—that you had eaten his salt—"

"Don't be absurd," said Devries, polishing the tray with a hunk of bread. "Ha! These Moors make good stew! So you don't want to go to Stamboul, eh? Will Rais Hassan listen to you?"

"He has already listened," said the Florentine darkly. "Most of the men aboard this galley of his will take his part; they're from Stamboul, and dislike Curtogalli, who is a Moor of Spain. If Curtogalli dies, Rais Hassan becomes leader of the fleet."

"Excellent!" said Devries, complacently. "You, with your talents, should be able to build well on such a foundation!"

Messer Bardi missed the sarcasm and appreciated the compliment blandly.

"The one trouble is," he said, "that we need someone aboard the admiral galley for a certain purpose."

He paused. Devries grinned. We! The word was eloquent. The whole project had been discussed, and some sort of plan made tentatively.

"I presume that much of the scheme must depend on the details of Curtogalli's plan for tonight—"

"Which we'll not know until Rais

Hassan returns from the council. Then, we may count you in with us?"

"Conditionally," said Devries coolly. "I want no share of the reward for Curtogalli's head. I do want the release of Countess Alix."

Bardi fingered his smooth chin. Obviously, he doubted such lack of self-interest. Devries read his expression aright, and went on quickly and shrewdly.

"Look you! There's reward enough for me. You know her wealth. Eh?"

"Oh, I see!" The Florentine chuckled. "You're not such a dunce after all! Yes, yes, it can be arranged. Let me handle the matter."

Liar and rogue! thought Devries to himself. The man was false to the core. Let him handle it, let him promise anything—ha! Two could play that game. Roger Devries began to get interested in the business, now that he could see a bit into it.

A roar of voices came from the deck, the pound of hasty feet. In upon them burst Rais Hassan, livid with fury and chagrin. He burst forth in a torrent of French.

"Small time to talk. The galeasse sails in an hour—ha! The Englishman!"

"Is with us." Bardi spoke rapidly, while the renegade stood glaring. "His price is the woman you hold for Stamboul; the Countess Alix. Grant it, grant it! She'll be of no importance, once Rome falls to you."

"I will not!" erupted Rais Hassan with gusty fury. "I mean to have her for myself. If this accursed Englishman thinks—"

"Come outside." Bardi took his arm, and directed a sly wink at Devries. "The air is clearing, the coast is in sight, and if I point out one little fact to you, then you may change your mind."

Rais Hassan let himself be argued out of the cabin, and the door closed.

DEVRIES smiled grimly. He was not deceived by the Florentine's pretence; he knew what that man was even now whispering in the renegade's ear. Promise anything, anything! Later, the Englishman could be killed easily, once Curtogalli could not protect him. Use him, kill him, take the woman desired!

The two came back inside. Rais Hassan was all wreathed in amiability now; he wasted no words, but came directly to the point.

"Good! It is settled. You shall have the woman; I'll set her ashore with you here. Now for the plans. Messer Bardi, there's no time to lose! As I say, the galeasse sails in an hour, under command of Curtogalli himself, with a crew of picked men—we have enough former Christians to fill her decks and avert suspicion, while others remain hidden below. She goes direct to Padiglione and anchors in the port, about sunset. The villa of the pope is two miles from the town."

Devries spoke suddenly. "Have you knowledge of the place?"

"Plenty of that," and Rais Hassan laughed. "Some of our men are from the locality; my rowing master was born there! Not a strip of coast in Italy, but we have slaves or soldiers who know it."

Renegades, obviously, had their uses.

"Curtogalli will take his men ashore, fifty of them, an hour before the dawn," went on Rais Hassan. "He'll go straight to the pope's villa, attacking at dawn. There is to be no great retinue with the pope; merely a few friends and secretaries and guards. They'll be cut down before they can get out of the gates, the pope will be seized. The others aboard the galeasse, hearing the signal shots, will then land and destroy the town. Curtogalli meets the rest of the fleet off the Tiber mouth, and pushes straight up the river for Rome."

"Before he gets there," said Devries, "warning will have been given."

"But he'll have the pope in his hands, and panic will do the rest."

Devries nodded. A good plan; it could not fail. Especially with a few traitors in Rome itself. Rais Hassan turned to the Florentine.

"There's the plan, Messer Bardi. Speak up, if you've anything to say; I see no way of taking any action."

"But I do." Bardi laughed. His soft, persuasive tones rang with assurance. "For you, for us, the plan is perfect! It could not have been better had we ourselves arranged it!"

"In the name of Allah, explain!" burst out the renegade, impatiently.

"Curtogalli goes with fifty men to the pope's villa, leaving the rest to loot the town when the firing starts. He does not go there until nearly dawn. He does not attack until dawn." Bardi chuckled. "How many men have you aboard here?"

"Two hundred at the oars, slaves; three hundred or more fighting men. But Curtogalli takes no slaves on the galeasse. He'll have a thousand men aboard her."

"Let him, let him; it should not worry us, since they'll be at the town, and he'll be two miles away at the villa—with only fifty men!" Bardi laughed again, softly, confidently. "Here's your action, if you're the man for it. When night falls, leave here under oars alone—send the other ships to lie off the Tiber mouth. Head straight in for the coast. Before midnight, land with two hundred men, a few miles above Padiglione. You'll have men who know the roads and the country for guides."

"Yes, yes?" Rais Hassan was tensed, eager, breathing hard. "And then?"

"It's very simple. Assign fifty men to the villa and the pope. With the rest, lie in wait for Curtogalli and his fifty. You'll have three times their number, men all devoted to you. Ambush him; fall upon him and slay! He and his fifty will suspect nothing. At the same moment, let your fifty strike at the villa. You see?" Bardi made an eloquent gesture. "Curtogalli dies. You become admiral of the fleet. You replace him, the pope is in your hands, you carry out the rest of his plan, join the fleet, and strike at Rome! The city will be yours before sunset tomorrow."

RAIS HASSAN caught his breath. His fierce eyes glowed; he clawed excitedly at his red beard, a blaze in his face.

"Ah, ah! You have genius!" he exclaimed admiringly. "Each man armed with pistols or arquebus; ha! That accursed arrogant Moor will be blasted at the first fire, and easily finished! Yes, it's perfect. Perfect! What about this Englishman?"

His eyes leaped to Devries.

"He'll be with Curtogalli," the Florentine rejoined suavely. "We need one man there we can trust. Suppose the plans are changed at the last moment? We must know it. We can leave nothing to chance."

"Nor can I," growled the corsair. "Suppose he betrays us?"

Devries spoke up, coolly.

"You have sense, Rais Hassan; use it. I want the Countess Alix and her wealth. Curtogalli refuses her to me, is determined to send her to Stamboul. Well! Nothing else counts with me. You give her to me, and I'm your man."

The scowling features of the renegade cleared.

"Right. That arrogant Spanish Moor has hung himself; with me, with Bardi whom he intends for Stamboul, and with you, his friend, on account of the woman. His stubborn vanity passes all bounds!"

"Obviously," said Devries. His firm, uncompromising mien was impressive. "You'll come to the villa by some road from the north. Good. I'll be able to warn you if plans are altered. It's not likely Curtogalli will take me to the villa with him; if he offers, I'll refuse. When you come along to the town, with the pope in your hands, I'll raise the cry for you. Curtogalli's men won't know what's happened until too late. You can take the galeasse and they'll be at your mercy—they'll have to join you."

"You, too, evidently have your value," said Rais Hassan, beaming.

"Look you, one last word!" put in Messer Bardi earnestly. "Remember this one thing; it's all important, Rais Hassan. Whatever you do, don't let the pope escape your hands! Who holds the pope, holds Rome. If he escapes you, any effort upon the city is useless. Grip him, and you have the city paralyzed, panic-struck, helpless!"

This was obvious enough. Messer Bardi, Devries shrewdly perceived, was giving good advice. Probably the Florentine had reasons of his own for hoping the mad scheme might succeed. Who holds the pope, holds Rome! True, doubly true. The success of the whole intent depended on this one point.

"Agreed, then. I'll have a word with Countess Alix," said Devries coolly, and rose. "Then I must rejoin Curtogalli. All's understood?"

"Aye," said Rais Hassan. "You'll warn us of any change in plans? We'll depend on you heavily for that."

"I'll do better," said Devries. "Consult with your men who know the coast and the roads. Tell me where you'll make your landing. I'll slip away from the galeasse and come to meet you, either at the landing or on the road to the villa."

"Excellent! Better and better!" exclaimed the renegade. But he exchanged one swift glance with the Florentine, and it gave away his thought to Devries. An easy matter to cut down the Englishman or slip a dagger into him, and have him out of the way.

"I'll send you word before the galeasse sails," went on Rais Hassan. "You'll come to meet us, then; we'll know definitely whether the plans remained unchanged."

"Agreed," said Devries, and left the cabin.

HE WENT to that of the Countess Alix. An Arab on guard outside her door saluted him and stepped aside. Knocking, he walked in at her command, and closed the door.

"Well?" she demanded, staring at him. "Ah, God! You look so hard, so stern—"

"Bah! I've been lying my head off, and it disgusts me," snapped Devries.

"Look you! I've cast the die, win or lose. With luck, I'll save the pope, save Rome, defeat this damnable conspiracy—but at a cost. Think well, and make decision, for I'll do as you say! If I go ahead with it, I see no hope for us, for you, for me; no escape. I'll make the effort, yes; some way may occur to me later. But I see none, to be frank, at present. Shall I go ahead or not?"

She stood white, stricken, eyes ghastly upon decision. Upon them dinned the roar of voices, of men at work and bustling, through the three ships. His blunt, forthright words drove into her with harsh emphasis. Her decision—for her to say! It came hard. She must damn herself and him; yet she must. She had no choice.

She came to him, put out her hands to him, and kissed him on the lips.

"There is my answer, dear knight," she said quietly. "Be noble!"

Devries drew a quick breath. "That's a motto worth the earning," he said, and caught her to him. "If I can, I'll come for you at sunrise, or before; at the worst, I'll come to die with you. Be noble! Good words, hard words, brave words."

He kissed her again, held her against him for a moment, and then went.

CHAPTER VI

THE Venetian galeasse, crowded with men, forged slowly, steadily, toward the blue coast of Italy. She was not a fast sailer, but no speed was desired now.

Under the sun-awning on the sterncastle sat Curtogalli, Devries and certain of his chief men clustered around; he was very merry and eager, as were they all, with high adventure spurring them on. Only Devries sat in glowering silence.

Word had come to him as promised. Rais Hassan would land at a cove four miles north of Padiglione; his galley would wait there. The highway ran south from there to town, passing the villa of Leo X on the way—a high villa above the shore, walled and gated, marked by tall cypress trees. It could not be missed. It stood alone.

"Why so dour, Englishman?" demanded Curtogalli with a laugh. "You sit silent and your eyes are murderous. Not thinking of me?"

Devries looked up, and his face cleared.

"No, not of you," he said with truth. He had been thinking of Messer Bardi of Florence. "Of a man whom I hope some day to kill."

"Then you'll need weapons," said Curtogalli, laughing. "I've brought you the best we have; a sword better than your own, at least, for it was forged of Toledo steel, and chain mail to match. It's all awaiting you below. Not that you'll need it tonight, Allah be praised! You can wait here aboard the ship, until our business is finished."

Devries nodded to this, without comment. To those around, Moors, Tunisians, Arabs, renegades, he was as an honored guest, a friend and brother of their master. Chivalry still existed; the hatred felt by Moslems toward Christians was not yet the bigoted, fanatic obsession it was to become a century later. And the knowledge that he was about to betray the friendship of Curtogalli, could not but render Devries gloomy; yet there was no other course.

"If I can, I'll come for you at sunrise . . ."

The arms were brought; his eye kindled to the fine steel of the sword, to the fine steel links of the mail, and the light, strong helm. He accepted them with fitting thanks, but he took small joy in them or anything else. He was struggling with his own problem now — how to accomplish what he must do.

And slowly, surely, the answer came to him. The one thing he had overlooked, forgotten, taken into no account!

THE sun went his westering way, the galeasse forged steadily on, the coast grew into blue hills against the sky, and Italy drew close. To the north lay Padiglione; the ship would strike it from the south, as though bound north to Livorno or Genoa. Sunset, said Curtogalli, would see them in the tiny harbor, no more than a cove at the river mouth.

And, as the time drew near, as a fishing boat or two broke the water horizon with brown sail, all traces of the corsairs vanished. By the hundreds, the eager sons of Islam filed below, with jests and laughter. Two small boats towed astern. On deck appeared a crew which to even an official inspection would assuredly be Venetian, or at least Christian. They were all renegades, men of every nation bordering the tideless sea, who had joined the corsairs for loot, if not for Allah; and they were carefully tricked out in Venetian costume.

Curtogalli, who disdained such disguise, remained out of sight in the cabin, whence he could give orders at will. Devries remained on deck, with a hooded cloak over his helm and coat of chain-mail. He had lost his gloom, now. Calculating his chances well, he was suddenly assured that destiny must serve him this night.

Sunset was at hand. The cove opened, the beach with its nets and boats, the little town built around the river-mouth. There was a great stir ashore as the galeasse headed in, but it quickly died. Sight of the Lion of St. Mark and the Cross on the big sails gave reassurance and quelled alarm. Curtogalli laughed and beckoned two of his men.

"You're both Italians by birth—anchor off those fishing wharves, take one of the boats, and go ashore. Tell any story that suits you. All I want to know is whether the pope has arrived at his villa. Bring back the word quickly."

On this point of suspense, indeed, hung all the plans. If the conspiracy were well guided, if Leo X had indeed arrived as scheduled, then all was well. If not, Curtogalli must make other arrangements.

There was no need to send ashore, however. Barely had the anchor plunged down, than a dozen boats pushed out to come alongside, laden with fruit and fish and grapes to sell the Venetians. None were allowed on board, but eager barter took place, news was exchanged, voices rang high. And the corsairs, in gleeful Arabic, muttered among themselves and pointed out likely houses for sacking at daylight.

Presently the information came. All was well. The pope himself had come that day to his villa, and the town was looking forward to a season of prodigality and blessings. Curtogalli, dipping his hand in the dish—they were at the evening meal—grinned at Devries and the others around.

"So! Praise to Allah, all goes well. Tell them to sheer off, that we have sickness aboard. Tomorrow will be time enough—there'll be more news then than they wot!"

Jests flew high and fast. But Devries, to whom this jesting over the fate of all Christendom brought little mirth, stood up, and Curtogalli understood his thought, as he spoke curtly.

"Give me a place to sleep," he said, "where I'll not be disturbed."

"Aye, comrade," said the Moor. "This is not your affair. Where you will."

"Then I'll curl up on deck in the stern. There's a pile of canvas by the rudder post. I'll not see you again until you return. May you have all the luck you deserve!"

"May Allah grant it!" said Curtogalli, and Devries went out.

DARKNESS was closing down now, the stars were out, all was quiet; but the corsairs down below stirred not. As he went aft along the lengthy waist, Devries heard the leaders discussing the orders. All hands sleep until an hour past midnight; then the shore party under Curtogalli would leave. The two trailing boats were in under the stern quarter.

But midnight would be too late for Roger Devries.

He made his place amid the pile of canvas, and stretched out, after removing helm and mailcoat and sword. Three persons entered into his problem: Pope Leo, Curtogalli, and Countess Alix. The end did not particularly matter, if he saved the first two from enemies and treachery. Fifty thousand ducats for Curtogalli's life—it revolted him. For himself, he had been too close to death all his life to worry greatly about it now. If he could do what was his to do, he could well afford to die with the Countess Alix.

Presently it came clearer in his mind. He rose and looked around. This high stern was deserted. The watch were all on the forecastle, closest to shore as the ship tugged at her anchor on the imperceptible ebb tide or current. A rope ladder had been put out in readiness. It was for him as well as for the others. Why not?

He seized the moment with its sudden thrill of a way opened. A rather simple, straightforward sort of man, this Roger Devries, unworried that the destiny of the world was hanging on his actions this night.

Haze in the air, high haze in the sky, nearly hiding the stars and darkening the water. Not a soul observed him or heard him as he descended the ladder and quietly laid his arms in the bottom of the boat. A large boat, designed to carry men ashore. He cast off the line, and the boat melted into the obscurity of the waters.

Once the galeasse was beyond his sight, he knew he was beyond her sight. An oar at the stern, and he dared to scull a little against the current, heading now for the few lights of the town. The shore drew nearer. The boat at last scraped the beach, and he stepped out to the shingle. Ashore, and free!

"Thank God!" he breathed, fervently.

Stooping, he sent out the boat with a long, strong shove, sent her swirling out and out. She would be found, later, when Curtogalli came to go ashore and missed her. It would forefend discovery of his escape, perhaps.

He donned his helm and mailshirt, buckled on his sword, and fumbled in his pockets. Curtogalli had not been

"Good evening, signores. I am come from the Venetian ship, and I desire a guide to the pope's villa."

niggardly; gold coins clinked dully, and he got one out. Free! The realization dinned at him, filled his brain, coursed in his veins, as he made his way toward the lights. A tavern, there, with men drinking and talking.

HE WALKED in and stood blinking at them, and they at him.

"Good evening, signores. I am come from the Venetian ship, and I desire a guide to the pope's villa." As he spoke, he showed the coin. Several men leaped up. Beckoning one who looked more intelligent than the rest, Devries was on his way in two minutes. The man plied him with eager questions about the Venetian ship, to which he answered little.

His guide rattled on. The pope loved sea fishing, and was going to spend much of his time out at the sport. He had commanded a boat for morning, in fact; whereat Devries smiled grimly to himself.

"There'll be no fishing in the morning," he said. "When we reach the villa, I'll send you back with a message to the captain of the Venetian galeasse. Instead of fish, you'll have corsairs."

"Impossible! They are swept away—"

"They are landing at dawn. I go to warn the pope," said Devries sternly.

His guide babbled with terror, but he heartened the man and questioned him. There was but the one road to the north, he found; he could not miss the galley of Rais Hassan.

It was not yet midnight when the villa appeared ahead and its lights showed that the folk were up and about. At the gates, a guard challenged.

"An English knight, from the Venetian ship in the harbor, to see His Holiness," said Devries, and turned to the man. "Here's your promised pay. Now go back, take a boat out to the galeasse, and tell her captain about guiding me here." Devries had altered all his plan on the spur of the moment. Let Curtogalli know the truth!

"Tell him that Rais Hassan and a pirate crew are already landed in the cove four miles north, with intent to kill him and to surprise the pope—he will understand."

"But, lord, how do you know this—"

"Never mind! Off with you!"

Devries was admitted to the villa grounds, on his plea of urgent news. Torches were lit. He strode forward to the steps, where a number of men came forth, staring curiously at him. That the pope was among them, he had no doubt.

"I come with warning, signores," he exclaimed abruptly. "You've not a moment to lose; mount and ride for your lives! Corsairs are landed in the cove to the north. They intend to seize the pope, if he be here, and then to mount the Tiber to Rome. Curtogalli and six or seven thousand men are at hand."

"Curtogalli!" Voices of alarm broke out. "But he is destroyed—"

"He is not destroyed. He is close," said Devries. "His whole fleet is bearing in toward the land. Ride for Rome and close the gates! There are traitors inside who are in league with the corsairs. Quickly!"

Warning enough. A sharp, imperative voice of terror leaped out, giving orders. Men began running to the stables, torches flitted, the group at the entrance scattered. Devries was forgotten, as panic took hold on all those men and spread like wild fire.

The pope saved from the trap, Curtogalli saved from treachery! As Roger Devries melted into the darkness, he felt a warm rush of confidence, of assurance, of joy in work well done. He had spoiled the great scheme of Curtogalli, but he had made amends by saving the Moor's life; and he was more than satisfied.

As he looked back before the night swallowed up the villa, he was aware of a pound of hooves, of shrill alarmed voices, and knew that his work there was done. Now remained the sterner work ahead.

He faced forward to it, in the darkness.

CHAPTER VII

THE road wound along the shore; scent of the salt sea, of olive trees and chestnuts, drifted along its course. The sense of loneliness increased unbearably. All sounds had died out behind, and the darkness made the rough road slow going.

Four miles of it. In those four miles, temptation tugged and swayed at Devries.

He had done his work. Curtogalli was warned. Rais Hassan would find the bird flown, the trap useless. The pope was spurring for Rome and safety. Why, then, go on to danger and probable death? Morning would bring safety, all enemies flown over the horizon. Why not await it? One woman more or less . . .

Devries strode on. A few days previously he might have entertained the thought, but not now. Those few hours aboard the galley with the Countess Alix had revolutionized all his ideas of her; he had gained an insight into her which left him astonished and fiercely jubilant. The woman, the one woman in all the world!

As for going to death, he would go to it gladly enough with her; but he was going to something else. All the future must march upon the events of this night. He wanted ten minutes aboard that galley, and the right man; then he would have a chance, at least, of success.

Rais Hassan, he figured, would be slow in learning that the bird had flown, that his trap had failed both victims. He would not get back to his galley much before sunrise, if then; a strange road made slow marching, as Devries was now learning. Yes, there would be a chance, a slim chance—

He halted suddenly. All his meditations went flittering. From somewhere close ahead in the obscurity he caught a voice in Arabic.

"Ma'ash' Allah! May the infidels who made this stony road rest forever in hell!"

Rais Hassan's men! Despite his startled, poised alarm, Devries grinned at the words. The corsairs had come as they were, bare-footed; and this road was undeniably stony underfoot. So much the slower marching, then.

Swiftly, Devries shrank in among the brush beside the road. The company obviously had been resting. Now an order came, was passed along; they were taking the road again, unhurried.

"If that accursed English infidel has tricked us," came the growl of Rais Hassan, I'll have him flayed and then impaled alive!"

"You can't expect him until later," came another voice. "This night is dark, the road strange. Mustapha has orders to await us?"

"Aye. He's camped ashore, the galley moored to the rocks. Close up, there! Close up, everyone!"

Devries waited motionless, held his very breath. The odor of unwashed bodies came to him, a jingle of arms, the sluff-sluff of feet, low cautious imprecations. Almost within arm's reach, the files of corsairs trooped past in the darkness. Still Devries waited, to give any stragglers plenty of time to pass.

Mustapha, probably the lieutenant left in charge, camped ashore with the remaining portion of the crew! That was good news. Guards would be posted, of course. There, all by now! With pulses athrob, Devries stepped out into the road and hurried on, sword loose in scabbard, senses straining against possible peril. But none came.

How far had he come? Two miles, three—difficult to say. As he strode on, he sent his thoughts back, with deliberate effort. Yes, he could remember the overseer who had charge of the slaves at the benches. No soldier at all; work with the oars demanded specialized skill. A fat Turk and hairy, heavy with the lash, cruel beyond belief to the poor devils chained to the ash benches. The name—ah! Murad. That was it. Murad, and his brutal lash tipped with bits of lead. Murad!

In this man now lay all the hope of Roger Devries.

HE WENT on watchfully, as fast as he could cover the stony road, poised to catch any warning from ahead. The time seemed interminable, the road endless. Waves, sucking at the rocks, sounded from his left; close to the water, now. Then he caught it—a low hum of voices, a stir, a confused sound of men.

Devries halted suddenly, so suddenly that his scabbard and mail-shirt clashed. A voice not three feet away spoke out.

"Eh? By Allah, who's there?"

"Silence, fool!" muttered Devries in Arabic. "Is that you, Ali?"

"No; it's Kaireddin."

"Did Murad come ashore?"

"That fat capon? No chance. He's snoring under the forepeak—"

The low voice ended in a gurgle, as Devries found his man; the gurgle died, as the shortened sword slipped home. Devries could take no chances now, could entertain no mistaken ideas of mercy with these wild beasts. He had come to grips at last, and death would take the slowest to strike.

The camp was a little way off; this man Kaireddin had evidently been a guard posted on the road. Knowing that discipline would be very slack, Devries was not worried over the absence of the man being noted. From his victim, he took a long dagger, with a grunt of satisfaction, then turned his attention to the shore and ship.

Great rocks studded the shore hereabouts. The camp, as he presently made out, was in a sandy niche among the rocks. Skirting it carefully to the left, he found that the rocky outcrop ended abruptly, beyond doubt in deep water, since the galley was drawn up slap against the rocks and made fast bow and stern.

He reconnoitered, weighing his chances as he made out the details in the darkness. How far the night had gone, he could not tell; it must now be well past midnight, at least. He found himself close to the bow of the galley, here. The stern, also moored to the line of rocks, was close to the camp; a mutter of voices came from there. Some of the crew might be still aboard in the high stern.

"That settles it, then," he reflected. "I'll have to stick to my first idea about Murad. Too bad! To cut her lines and let her go adrift in the darkness would be a splendid stroke; but it can't be done by one man."

Murad was asleep in the forepeak, the guard had said. Gaining the galley's side, Devries found her moored with only fenders against the rock, so close that one might step to the rail. In the long, low waist slept the rowers, the slaves chained to their benches for life; the stench of them rose to him, the sound of their snoring, their groans, their restless stirrings.

The bow, however, seemed deserted. Next moment he had stepped aboard.

Now he was safe from notice or molestation; every man who could had gone ashore, except the one man whom he most sought, whom he must find. Not for himself, not for any speech with this Murad; but for that which Murad carried at his girdle, the badge of his office, the symbol of his rule. The heavy master-key which fitted the locks of every slave at the benches. Only death would part the Turk from that key.

DEVRIES came to the narrow runway that entered the forepeak, and then halted. Murder a man sleeping? He could not do it. Besides, in that pitch blackness too many things might happen. All now depended on success at this one point; he dared not risk failure. He stooped, and sent in his voice.

"Murad! Murad! Waken, Murad!"

A growl responded, a sleepy word.

"Aye! What is it?"

"Rais Hassan is back. He wants you instantly."

Another growl. A stir. "May Allah reward him with a century in hell! I come."

After a moment, he came, a huge bulking figure stooping to emerge from the runway. Stooping, and coming erect no more; stooping, and plunging forward headlong to die on the deck as the dagger smote him. A sure blow, a true blow, a strong blow. Without even a groan, the Turk collapsed on the deck.

Devries knelt, rolled him over, and explored the massive shape. On the belt hung the key, by its chain; he loosened the belt, and had it. With a leap of his heart, he turned back toward the rower's benches and gained the runway or planked walk that ran the length of the waist, between the benches.

Now, under his breath, he spoke softly.

"Is there any Christian man here?"

He repeated the question as he passed. A naked form stirred and sat up.

"Aye! Who asks? What is it?"

"Silence!" Devries halted, crouched. "Who are you?"

"Jean Leschamps of Marseille, or I was."

"Will you fight if I release you?"

The slave caught his breath. "Fight? Aye, by God I will!"

"Careful, then—no noise! One sound, and we're all lost. Were you at an oar when the *nef* was taken a couple of days back?"

"Aye. Ah! I know you now! The English knight who fought—"

Desperately, Devries covered the man's mouth with his hand.

"Not a sound, I tell you! Let me do the talking. Reach over your irons."

The amazed, bewildered Frenchman was freed. Devries crouched beside him and put the master-key in his hand.

"There are others who'll fight?"

"Some, yes. Some are past fighting. Others would snitch to curry favor—"

"Do you know where the weapons are kept?"

"Yes. Forward."

"Pick your own friends, men who'll fight." Devries spoke softly, rapidly. "Don't make a sound, don't utter a cry, but wait until I give the alarm. Then join me in the stern. First, assign two of your friends to cut the bow line. We'll have to fight in order to cast off the line in the stern. Do you understand?"

"Yes, yes!" muttered Leschamps fervently. "God bless you! I didn't think you were real—I thought you might be some angel—you can trust me to be careful! I know the right ones to pick, and all we ask is to put a blade through one of these devils before we die!"

"Enough. Were any guards left aboard?"

"The lady's cabin has a guard, yes. The Florentine, none."

Devries had forgotten Messer Bardi. Now he laughed softly, grimly, and with a final warning, moved on aft.

FROM the rowers' benches and this central planked walk, the cabins opened directly. The stern deck, above, was the danger point; guards were there, and on the rocks ashore, where the camp was. A low buzz of voices sounded. Somebody yawned.

"Ah! Look at the east—there's the false dawn! Daylight will soon be here, and the morning prayer."

Somebody laughed and made a jest, and Devries found himself at the entrance to the cabin passage. A figure moved in front of him.

"Stay out of here, comrade!" came the careless words. "You know the orders—"

The voice pointed the blow, the reaching hand. Devries had the guard by the throat, and plunged home his dagger. The blow missed. The guard wore a steel-mesh shirt. The gripping fingers sank in the sinewy throat, however, and the second blow drove home.

The guard sagged down. Working swiftly, Devries stripped off his chain shirt, took his sword-belt and helm, and went on. He knew now where he was; a moment, and he found the locked door of Countess Alix. He scratched on the wood and heard her voice.

"Who is it?"

"I."

A low cry; hands fumbled at the bolts, the door swung open. He had reached her.

CHAPTER VIII

"NO NOISE, no noise!"

Desperately, freeing himself from her ecstatic embrace, Devries took the girl in his arms for a brief moment. Then he pressed his burden upon her.

"Here, get into this mail-shirt, take this sword. We'll have to fight for it—"

"Ah!" She recoiled from the touch. "Warm and sticky—it's blood!"

"Not yours," said he grimly. "Can you fight?"

"If I must, I suppose I can. Help me with it. It's not sunrise yet—why have you come? How did you get here?"

Devries laughed at her eager flow of questions, as he aided her to get the chain-shirt on.

"All's done," he rejoined under his

breath. "The pope's riding hard for Rome. We might slip ashore, but we'd be run down in no time; Rais Hassan may be back at any moment now. I've loosed some of the slaves. Our one sure chance, win or lose all, is to cast loose the galley, To do that, we must put up a fight. If we can get her away from the shore, Rais Hassan and his men are lost, and we're safe."

"Oh!" A low, swift cry broke from her as she comprehended. Then she changed, quieted and came to him in the darkness, her hand on his arm. "Tell me. You saw the pope?"

"Yes, I suppose it was he," said Devries.

"And you came back here. You might have gone with him—"

"Bah! I keep my promises; don't mention it again. You'd have done the same."

"Not I!" She laughed softly. "At least, not yesterday. Today, life's different. But I warn you, don't trust Messer Bardi! I heard him talking with Rais Hassan. They're friends. Hassan meant to kill you and said so. Bardi only laughed."

"Yes. I don't like his laugh. Well, never mind him; he's asleep."

"Very well. Tell me what to do."

"Use your sword on the line from the stern to the rocks. It'll take some cutting. I'll cover you while you do it."

She assented; they gripped hands; then he drew open the door and stepped out.

"Wait. Don't move till I return," murmured Devries.

He headed aft. Catching a dim clank of chains, a vague stir on the benches, he muttered the name of Leschamps. The Frenchman came to him with a low, fierce word.

"Aye, lord! Twelve are freed. Two have gone for arms, two more to cut the bow line to shore, or cast it off. I'm freeing others."

"We'll need every man," rejoined Devries. "I'll wait, aft, until you're ready, or until some alarm is caused."

He rejoined the Countess Alix. The haze had vanished now; a vague gray was stealing over everything, token of the coming dawn. The two waited, weapons ready, in silence.

Came a sudden clank of chains, and a mutter of voices from the slave-benches. An officer on the stern deck gave a sharp order.

"Ali! See what those dogs are up to; fighting, perhaps. Tell Murad to lay the whip on them. The lazy Turk is probably snoring."

Devries touched the girl. "Ready! The rope, mind, and nothing else."

A step sounded on the ladder. A man leaped down to the deck; as he landed, the sword of Devries cut him down. His shrill death-cry gave alarm, and Devries was up the ladder with a leap. Yelping voices from the waist told that the slaves were ready.

Devries had one glimpse of the Countess Alix, making for the shore line; then he turned and faced the group of corsairs dimly visible. He stood grimly silent, while they cried out questions, demands, orders. As the girl's sword began to hack at the stout hawser, voices of alarm went up. An Arab leaped toward her across the deck, but Devries met him midway, and the keen Toledo swung and clashed. That man died.

"To me, Leschamps!" lifted the shout of Devries.

Half a dozen men here before him, around him; cries of alarm rising on shore, in the camp, a wild howl of naked men from the waist. Devries waited no longer, but hurled himself at the group of corsairs. In the obscurity they were uncertain, bewildered. He cut down one, and another. For a moment, he had visions of clearing the whole stern, single-handed, until a cry from the girl drew him around.

TWO men had leaped aboard from shore — guards there — and were rushing at her. Barely in time, Devries came leaping in between. A sword-point found his body, but the chain-mail saved him from the thrust; as he staggered, the second man came diving in with a sweep of scimitar at the knees. Barely did Devries ward the blow. Then he had his balance again, and the Toledo blade swung and swung, cutting through steel cap and skull beneath like cardboard.

An instant of breathing-space. The galley was swinging out at the bow; slaves had oars against the rocks, pushing her out. There was a rush of men from the camp, a din of shrill yells. Half a dozen came tumbling aboard, just as the Countess Alix cried out.

"Finished! It's cut!"

Dawn was brightening. Another group came tumbling aboard, jumping the widening gap, throwing their comrades here into confusion. More took the leap, landing all asprawl on deck. A score of corsairs here now, and thrusting forward at Devries. One reached him, and yelled to Allah as the Toledo bit into him. Another flung himself bodily in and gripped Devries about the waist, dagger plunging vainly at the steel shirt. The sword-hilt smashed up into his face, smashed him backward, beat him away, and the point took him as he fell.

Sword in one hand, dagger in the other, Devries faced the rush; but here Leschamps intervened.

A wild and terrible howl, the ravening scream of wild beasts, pealed up as the freed slaves reached the stern-deck. Gaunt men, naked and bearded, armed with anything that had come to hand, they hurled themselves at the corsairs. Instantly there was a furious mêlée, pierced by the yells of fury and dismay from ashore, as the men in camp realized that the ship was swinging out. A few more came leaping over the rail. One missed, then another, and went down.

But here along the stern-deck swept death and passions let loose, as the slaves killed and were killed. Devries flung himself into the midst of the struggle, seeing that these naked men could scarce hope to face the armored Moslems. His voice rallied them, he surged into the forefront and led them, they gathered behind him and swept ahead in wild fury. They died fast, but they killed as they died, and the clanging, ringing Toledo crashed through helm and shield and armor.

Daggers bit, swords clashed, curved scimitars hacked and slashed. Devries was bleeding now, but the deck was clearing. Three or four corsairs remained in a knot, and he smashed straight at them. Steel whirled and clashed; the weight of his rush bore them back. A stiletto shivered against his steel shirt. Another stabbed into his neck. A scimitar cut across his chest vainly. The Toledo sang and crashed down again and again. But one man remained now, and him Leschamps took with a yell and a leap—

took him down, rolled over and over with him, and rose with red dagger and exultant shout. Clear!

At a price, however. The growing daylight revealed terrible things as Devries, sobbing for breath, leaned on his sword and glanced around. Many of the unarmed slaves had died there. Leschamps and half a dozen more stood triumphant, and others were coming from the benches as they were freed; but the wounded corsairs fought to the very death.

EVEN as Devries looked around, he caught a yell, a cry, and saw the Countess Alix go down as a wounded Arab leaped on her with steel flashing. Leschamps yelled and went in with a leap, and pinned the Arab to the deck, but as the girl came to her feet, unhurt, she cried out again.

"Look! They're coming aboard!"

So they were, indeed. They were coming over the rail as though by magic, half a dozen at once. Bows were twanging ashore; an arrow hit Devries between the shoulders, blunted on his chain shirt, but staggered him with the blow. And from ashore was going up a mighty shout, a wild pandemonium of voices—Rais Hassan was back with his full force, back in wrath and wild fury and insane rage!

They were coming aboard, yes. The slaves ran, hacking and thrusting, only to be cut down in their tracks. Half a dozen, a dozen—Arabs full armed from a small boat. And at the rail, helping them aboard, a man who had let down a rope to them—a man pallid and filled with terror, yet acting sharply enough in a pinch—Messer Bardi of Florence.

Bardi, a bloody stiletto in his hand, struck at her again, again.

To Devries, this moment was frightful. He seemed palsied, unable to move, as the corsairs came across the stern-deck with a rush, as the yelling slaves gathered to meet them, as the Countess Alix flew like a tigress at Bardi and cast off the ropes the Florentine had lowered. Then she slumped away, catching at the rail, and Bardi, a bloody stiletto in his hand, struck at her again, again—

With this, Devries found himself moving. What happened, he did not know; Bardi lay stretched on the deck, he was upholding Countess Alix, looking into her face, crying out her name.

"Not hurt, not hurt—much," she gasped. "The chain-mail saved me—ah! Look, look!"

It was the supreme moment, the moment of crisis. The galley had swung well out from the rocks, no others could come aboard; but the dozen men in armor were making sad havoc of the thronging slaves. With a groan, Devries loosed the girl and rushed into the brunt of the fray, cursing the traitorous Florentine who had helped these fresh men aboard.

Armed now from the dead on the deck, the slaves fought with ferocity equal to that of the Moslems, but they were not skilled in fighting. Devries turned the tide, stemmed the corsair rush, and stood like a rock with the Toledo swinging red in the white day-stream. In vain they hammered and slashed at him.

Their leader sprang in, a renegade like Rais Hassan, with a dazzling display of skill as his curved blade swung and bit and slashed. He, too, was clad in chain mail; the Toledo struck it and glanced away. A slash in return sent Devries reeling, and the Moslem yells pealed up—but next instant they died. For, as the renegade leaped in to deliver the finishing blow, Devries reached him with a backhand slash across the face, sudden and unexpected; then the point drove home to the throat, and finished it.

The others drew away. They had no escape now, for the galley had drifted well off the rocks; they were between the devil and the deep sea with a vengeance, and what was left of the slave-pack went at them with a will, Leschamps leading. Devries, too, strode in upon them, saved Leschamps from a Moor at his back, and got his dagger-point into the Moor.

A yell close beside him, a cry of warning from Leschamps—too late! A stricken Turk, writhing half upright, stabbed and stabbed again. His point caught Devries in the thigh, beneath the edge of the mail-coat, and went deep. Not until the sword-point went through his beard did he relax in death, and Devries, leaning on the reddened point, knew that he was out of this fight and any other for many a day. He staggered to the rail and collapsed as Countess Alix came running to his aid.

For a space he sat leaning against the bulwark, weak and sick, then rallied. She had bound up the hurt thigh with deft, swift fingers, and the blood was checked. Devries nodded to her, smiled faintly, and looked across the deck.

"It's over," she was saying, jubilant and betwixt tears and laughter. "Over, my dear, ended!"

ENDED, indeed. The last of the corsairs had leaped into the sea and was swimming for shore. The galley had drifted out so far that the arrows had ceased. The freed slaves, in a delirium of joy, were clearing the decks, flinging dead and dying over the side together, poniarding the wounded; no corsair was left alive on those red planks.

Leschamps, streaming blood from a dozen minor wounds, came up like a gaunt scarecrow, babbling almost incoherent French.

"A hundred and more of us, lord—we can work the ship, we can man the oars! She is yours. Give me your orders, and we obey."

Devries pulled himself up a little until he could see the shore, and smiled grimly. The corsairs were grouped there in utmost dismay; Rais Hassan and his men, set ashore, were caught in their own trap now; instead of raiding Italy, they would be raided by Italy with bitter vengeance.

"Won!" said Devries, and met the rapt gaze of the Countess Alix. "Won—we've done the impossible! We've won—"

He leaned back again weakly. One of the slaves, who were given wine rations by the corsairs, came running with a cup. Devries drank, and felt the wine, bitter as it was, give him new life. He put up a hand to the Countess Alix.

"Help me get on my feet. I can stand well enough—"

As she aided him up, a long, shrill cry came from forward. It was echoed all down the deck. The naked, gaunt men paused in their work and stood staring. Daylight had merged into sunrise now; the whole eastern sky was red.

"What is it?" demanded Devries, leaning against the rail. "What is it, Leschamps?"

The scarecrow Frenchman had turned livid beneath his bronze. He lifted a shaking, blood-smeared hand. His eyes were wild, staring; a frightful cry broke from a group of the ex-slaves. They, too, were staring.

Devries turned painfully. He saw the Countess Alix, white as death, sway a little and then catch herself. He followed her gaze, the gaze of them all, out to the rocky promontory that cut off the shore to the south from view.

Something had appeared there, just beyond the promontory. A ship, tall and high, oars flashing and dripping; a ship, heading in for them—

"The galeasse!" gasped Leschamps. "We're lost—lost—"

Lost, indeed. It was the Venetian galeasse of Curtogalli, and Devries felt his heart sink within him as she headed for them.

CHAPTER IX

THE deck of the galley was wrapped in stricken silence.

The silence was broken by sobbing voices, gusty heart-broken wails, wild fierce prayers and blasphemies; then staring silence fell again.

Gone now was any gleam of hope. Useless now to fight, impossible to run, escape to shore was cut off by the corsairs stranded there. Men dropped weapons and sank down, covering their faces; others, with streaming tears, sobbed out their lost hopes. But Devries, one arm about the Countess Alix, leaned with the other on his sword and stood gazing at the great gay ship.

Suddenly her oars poised, remained motionless. She lost way. A few hundred yards distant, she halted and hung, as though indecisive.

"He's there—in the bow," said the Countess Alix with white lips.

Devries had already seen him. The tall, soldierly figure of Curtogalli himself, regarding them, regarding the groups of corsairs ashore, unheeding their hoarse yells. The situation must have been very clear to him, in this moment; Rais Hassan ashore, the galley taken by her own slaves, the figures of Devries and the girl there at the rail.

"He knows by this time," said Devries grimly, "that I saved him from Rais Hassan—and lost him his prize. Well, my dear, kiss me again! After all, a man can die but once—"

The Countess Alix turned to him, and kissed him. Then she faced again to the great galeasse and the tall, swarthy figure in the bow.

Suddenly Curtogalli moved. He took off his Persian helmet and dropped it beside him, as though he wished to be recognized beyond any doubt. He waved his hand, as though in salute; he turned, and disappeared among those around him. The oars of the galeasse dipped. She swung slowly. She headed away. Her sails caught the shore-breeze and filled, the oars were taken in—and she stood away steadily, rapidly, heading into the horizon.

Devries was the only one who understood, when he realized that she was actually leaving. He lifted his sword and waved it, and sank back against the bulwark.

"Good man, true knight!" he said, with a gasp of emotional reaction. The girl looked at him, amazement in her eyes.

"He's leaving? Oh, it can't be true—why would he do that?"

Devries smiled. How much Curtogalli knew, how much he forgot, how much he had forgiven—no matter now. His arm tightened about the Countess Alix, and he smiled again as he met her blue eyes.

"Why would he do that? To pay his debts; his debts to Rais Hassan, and to me, and to you, perhaps. He pays them like a true and gentle knight, God rest him! And now, my dear, kiss me again—this time in joy, in victory, in the flush of sunrise that'll gild all the future for us—"

And Curtogalli went his ways, to fame, to glory, to honors, with his debts paid.

***Remember* "ROMAN HOLIDAY"?**

Don't Miss

"BARD OF BABYLON"

by A. Westcott McKee

NEXT MONTH

Thunder Bolt

by Kenneth P. Wood

Illustrated by MAURICE ARCHBOLD, Jr.

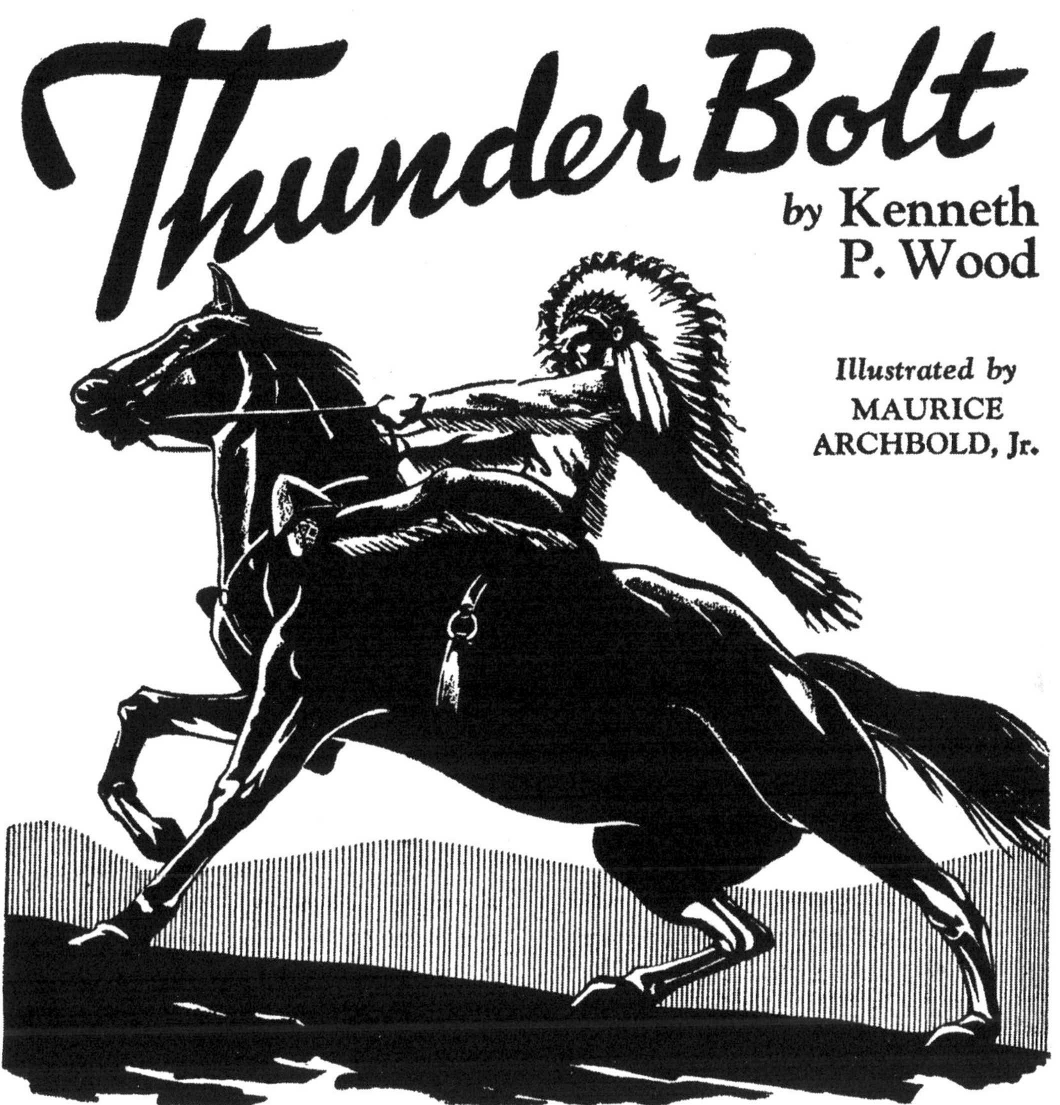

"SAY, you rookies don't know nothin' about smart hosses!" snorted the old campaigner, coming into the conversation suddenly. "If this old Seventh Cavalry ain't had the smartest hossflesh in the Dakotas in its day, I'll lose my ante. Smart hosses! Why, what about Old Baldy; and Comanche, Cap'n Keogh's mount, the on'y survivor of the Custer Massacre that was put on a pension at Fort Riley back in the Sioux Seventies. A lot different from the nags they issue to yuh nowadays.'

The speaker raised in his bunk, and vehemently spattered the barracks' stove with a spray of tobacco juice, while the recruits of Troop C were hushed with attention. The old trooper's reservoir of talk, made brimming by long silence, was beginning one of its periodic overflows.

"But there was another hoss belongin' to this troop that was smarter'n any of 'em, which we picked up durin' the Messiah craze and Sioux uprisin' in 1890, long before yore time in the outfit. We'd been follerin' a Injun trail for weeks and lived on boiled prairie dog and cactus salad, till one mornin' us boys jest up and pulled out for game country and meat. When we'd filled up a-plenty on buffalo hump and venison, we come back to camp with the redskin smell fresh out of our noses on'y to be ordered to hit the trail right off, for the hostiles was on the prod again.

"The hoss I'm referrin' to was rode by Jim Barker, who used to be a bugler in Troop C. Jim riz from the ranks to cap'n, and married a colonel's daughter, but he got bumped off in the Philippines in '98. We used to be bunkies, him and me. One of the squarest and nerviest boys that ever straddled a gov'ment mount.

"And do yuh know, he onct deserted on account of that hoss—and a man. The hoss was a sojer, but the man was a peak-nosed runt of a second lieutenant named Frank Ellis; all varnish and strut. The boys hated him like pizened dirt, and he got back at 'em every chance. Them was the wild and woolly days, I tell you! And the saddler in the case was one of the finest pieces of hossflesh that ever carried the U. S. brand. Ellis wanted him, and Barker got him. Then there was hell all around . . . 'specially for Jim.

"We got the hoss in a queer way. We was chasin' old Strike-the-Kettle, one of Sittin' Bull's leaders along the Upper Grand River. Barker and Ellis, and our troop, and a couple of others was ahead of the main command, keepin' an eye on the Injun rear. Right in the middle of a runnin' fight every red man disappeared; then, it was look out for an ambush. Our company was scattered, so the colonel sent Jim to a high ridge, a little ways ahead, to blow the recall.

"Barker was a reckless sort of kid in them days. He had a habit of gettin' there when he was sent, and Colonel Furey—Old Leather Breeches, the boys called him, for he was an old hand at the game, and a Injun fighter to his finger tips who swore in six languages—took a shine to Jim, and always wanted him around.

"Well, Barker was up there on the ridge tootin' away about twice as far ahead as he ought to have been, as usual, when 'way down in the brush he hears a crashin' and thrashin' as if an unruly cayuse was tearin' about. So he pulls his Colt and sends some slugs into the thicket just for luck. Well, sir! It was fairly alive with savages. They thought we saw 'em, and they scattered like a bunch of scared rabbits. There was Jim, six-shooter in one hand and bugle in the other, tootin' and shootin' away, when all of a sudden a beautiful big black hoss, with a painted brave on his back, broke from covert and headed straight for him. Our line was formin' a quarter of a mile back, when Old Leather Breeches got sight of the flyin' Injuns, and then he give us the charge, and away we went after 'em.

"WE COULD see the big black tearin' along toward Barker. The Injun on his back was a tall buck, wearin' a white ghost-shirt, with a war-bonnet of eagle feathers streamin' out behind, and he was layin' back on the reins, tryin' to stop. But on that brute's back he was helpless as a papoose in a rawhide cage. And the gait of that hoss was a sight to behold! It fairly made us yell. He was rangy and powerful built, and had the action of a thoroughbred. He was goin' like the wind, his head pushed far out, and him gatherin' and stretchin' as easy and graceful as a antelope. When he got in sight of our

"I've come after my hoss, sir," says Barker.

blue line he whinnered to us. That showed the wind he had. We was a-whoopin' it up to reach the reds before they got to cover, and the big black with his Sioux rider was headin' straight toward us. He dashed by Barker, and Jim took right after him. They had to cross a brushy hollow to reach us, and there the Injun tried to dismount—but he was goin' too awful fast. Then he raised his rifle and put the muzzle agin the mount's ear . . . but that minute Barker pinned him in the back. He yelled fierce and went over the black's head, while the hoss kept a-comin' our way. We opened ranks and let him through, with Barker at his heels.

"The bugler never was proud of that shot in the back, but we all declared that in our opinion any skunk who'd maim such a hoss just to escape capture deserved killin' with a pitchfork—shootin' was too good for him.

"After the line passed, the black wheeled and trotted up to Jim, whinnerin' and laughin' as on'y a happy hoss can. Jim was wanted at the front, and he had no time to waste. So he tucked his hank'chief under the saddlebow and turned the animal loose. As he did so he spotted the U. S. brand on the shoulder so he figgered it was a captured army hoss. When the mount heard the bugle so close he'd just grabbed the bit in his teeth and bolted. There was no danger of his runnin' away, so Barker left him and skipped to his post. Well, sir, that hoss made straight for the blue line, jammed into place, and through the whole fracas kept formation like a veteran. When we halted, he walked around among the boys, makin' friends with all of us, an' chawin' manes with our nags.

"The main part of the command caught up with us purty soon, but Jim had to stay with the colonel till we went into camp. The first thing he did was to go rustlin' around for that prize hoss of his'n. He found him at the officers' fire, with Ellis a-holdin' the bridle and the whole officers' mess standin' in admiration.

" 'I've come after my hoss, sir,' says Barker, s'lutin' Ellis.

" 'Yours!' barks Ellis, high and mighty.

" 'Yes, sir, I got him first,' says Jim. 'Here's my hank'chief I put under the saddle. See, it has my name and number on,' he explains, pullin' the hank'-chief out.

" 'What's that got to do with it?' snaps the shave-tail, squarin' hisself like he was Napoleon.

" 'I captured the hoss, lieutenant, and I think I ought to have him,' says Jim.

" 'You're lyin' to a officer. Do yuh know that?' growls Ellis. 'The hoss was runnin' loose when I got him. Go back to yore quarters . . . I'll report yuh for impertinence!'

"Now, half the company had turned in their saddles and saw Barker ketch the big black. Maybe Ellis didn't see it, but the hank'chief was there, and if he hadn't been such a selfish little whelp he'd 'a found out how it got under the saddle. Jim had to come away without the saddler, but he didn't give up—not by a damn sight. Next mornin' early he went to the colonel's headquarters. He said he wanted the hoss more'n anything in the world or he'd 'a backed away from Old Leather Breeches after he saw him. Barker laid on the sob stuff thicker'n fat on gov'-ment bacon. The old boy was fierce-lookin' anyhow, but when Jim went in he was writin' and wearin' glasses, which always made him look ten times harder. To make matters worse, he'd just got orders from General Miles he didn't like, and, altogether, he was purple in the face. Barker said he looked as savage as a grizzly with a trap on each foot. But it was go through with it or lose the hoss, so Jim says, easy-like:

" 'Colonel, I captured a hoss yesterday, and Lieutenant Ellis took him from me.'

"The old boy didn't like Ellis nohow. He thought he had a yeller streak and treated him accordin', and if you knowed Old Leather Breeches that'd mean a lot to you. But he liked the bugler in his gruff way. He give him a good word the day before, too, for uncoverin' the Sioux ambush.

" 'What, that black yuh chased into the lines yesterday?' roars the old man.

" 'Yes, sir,' says Barker, 'and I need him bad—mine's on three laigs every mornin'.'

"Then the colonel cussed till the tent shook. 'Go take yore hoss and keep him!' he bellers. 'Orderly, tell Lieutenant Ellis to report here at once!'

"WHAT Ellis got from Old Leather Breeches that mornin' we never knowed, but for a week after the young cub was actu'lly meek. So Barker brought the big black 'round to his hitchin' post and turned his old saddler over to the quartermaster.

"Thunder Bolt, Jim named his new mount for some reason of his own. The

Injuns had ganted him up purty bad, and his mouth was cut and tore from the Mex spade bit they'd used on him. But Jim patched him up, and fed him, and slicked him till he looked like a sultan's pet. In a week Thunder Bolt was the pride of the Seventh. I'd give a month's pay to shake hands with the man that trained him. The hoss knew every call before the bugle finished it, and never made a mistake. When a tangle come on parade, he was as worried as the file-closer hisself. At monkey drills and trick ridin' he was a wonder, and Jim was just risky enough to keep him company in anything he'd do. It was the show of the post to see them two get out of a evenin' and go through their capers. Even the colonel used to come out and watch 'em both and grin. If ever a man loved a hoss Jim Barker loved Thunder Bolt, and the old hoss made good every time.

"But Ellis, the dirty dog, was bent on gettin' Thunder Bolt by hook or by crook. His hungerin' eyes was follerin' him continually. Often on guard mount I've seen him turn in his saddle to watch the big black cuttin' corners and wheelin' and startin' as sober as a judge. It did Jim's kid heart good, too, to show the saddler off when Ellis was around. About the stables Ellis was forever pettin' the critter and fussin' over him. The on'y good thing I could say of the upstart was he knowed and respected genuine hossflesh. Dev'lish treatment, though, Jim got from Ellis after the mornin' in the colonel's tent. Ellis had laid a deep scheme to get Thunder Bolt, and he played it cruel hard. Barker's term run out that winter, and Ellis knowed it. He calc'lated that Jim'd up an' quit the service if it was made good and hot for him in the few months he had to serve. Thunder Bolt was gov'ment property, and if Jim left, Ellis could nail him right off. But the bugler called his bluff.

"Barker's life was worse than black slavery durin' the rest of the summer. He was on fatigue and night duty every time Ellis could put him there, and the dirtiest and most dangerous work the looey could find or invent was sent his way. One winter day while we was haulin' a Gatlin' and a Hotchkiss gun and some freight to Fort Yates, a six-mule team broke through the ice of a creek. As luck would have it, Jim was drivin', and Ellis was in charge. The little blaggard pulled his revolver and made Jim get down into the slush, waist-deep, to block up the wheels. Pneumony set in and nearly killed the lad.

"OUT of the hospital several months later came Barker, lookin' like a mortal wreck. It was the very day his term expired, and the poor devil said he guessed he'd quit the outfit and go home for a rest. But that afternoon he put his arm around my neck, for he was weak and wobbly, and we walked over to the stables to see Thunder Bolt. Well, sir, the old hoss knowed Jim's shadder the minute we entered the door. He whinnered and pawed in his stall, and when Jim went in beside him he snuffed all over him and rubbed his nose agin him as if it was just too good to be true that Barker'd come back. And Jim he just broke down, too.

"When we left the stable Jim started off without any help. 'Yer gettin' better purty sudden, ain't yuh?' I says to him.

"'I'm all better,' he answers with snap. 'I'm not goin' to the barrack just yet, old friend,' he blurts out, as he headed a different way.

"'Where yuh goin'?' I calls after him.

"'I'm goin' over to the sarjant's and enlist again.'

"And he did just that.

"Barker soon built up and got well and strong, in spite of the infernal abuse Ellis heaped on 'im. The lieutenant was surprised and disappointed when Jim re'nlisted, and started in to get even. But the bugler seemed to keep his heart up as long as he had Thunder Bolt to fuss over and talk to. The old feller seemed to know Jim was havin' a tough time of it, too, for every mornin' he'd whinner a welcome, and tuck his soft muzzle under Jim's arm in the gentlest way, as if tellin' him to 'buck up and never mind.' Things looked black for Barker, though, when Colonel Furey was called to Washington. The old man was a terror to Ellis and kept him in his place . . . but now Jim was in a bad way. A few days after Furey left, Jim went to Thunder Bolt's stall and found it empty. Ellis had taken him. Barker vowed to me then and there that he'd desert and take his hoss along.

"The chance Jim was waitin' for soon come. It was in the middle of a week-long snowstorm, and the stable sarjant got soused to the ears. We put him in his bunk, and Jim volunteered to take his place. Then when nobody was around he got some civvies he had ready, strapped a blanket on Thunder Bolt, and struck out into the blindin' snow. I didn't sleep much that night for thinkin' of Jim out in the blizzard. But I knowed he had a hoss under him with bottom that never was reached, and that would stick to him to the last ditch.

"There was heap big excitement when Barker and the hoss was missed the next mornin', and a mounted squad started out after 'em. But, hell! there wasn't a mount in the command that could keep Thunder Bolt in sight, let alone ketch him after eight hours' start. Nevertheless Barker was caught. The telegraph did it within a week. He was brought back, court-martialed, and got twelve months at hard labor, forfeited a year's pay, and, worst of all, lost Thunder Bolt for good. Ellis'd won out at last.

"A YEAR in the guardhouse ain't likely to make a man sweet-tempered or ready to forget a wrong. Jim came out busted from musician to a private, sick and discouraged. But he had one burnin' purpose in mind. I knowed, though he never talked about it, and that was to get square with Ellis. The lousy coyote knowed Jim had it in for him, and he took special care never to be caught alone. Barker wasn't a revengeful feller by nature, but he was on'y a kid then, half-crazy from abuse and the loss of his pet hoss. He could 'a killed Ellis easy enough, but that wouldn't satisfy Jim in the state of mind he was in. He wanted to fight him, and fight him to death. So things went on that way for a month or so, each watchin' the other, till one bloody day God A'mighty stepped between 'em, and tromped the looey out.

"A buck private forcin' a duel on a officer is no light matter, and it was the luckiest thing that ever happened to Barker when Troop C was sent out that winter to round up Big-Foot's band that had broken away from the Standin' Rock Agency and fled into the Badlands where they was ghost-dancin' and raisin' hell generally. Ellis was first

lieutenant then, and Cap'n Forsythe bein' sick, Ellis was in command. There was a lot of guessin' amongst the boys as to how he'd behave in leadin' a fight. The majority allowed Ellis was yeller all the way through . . . and the majority was right.

"We struck the Sioux trail and raised a covey of a hundred of 'em. They headed up a narrow gulch, and Ellis sent us right after 'em. We knowed that there was five hundred of the red devils in the vicinity, and while it was all right to pitch into the small bunch, it was a schoolboy trick to foller 'em up too close when they got into the narrow canyon. When the covey run away, though, Ellis thought he was whippin' 'em good, and as we reached the gulch he ordered us to break formation and dash through after 'em. It was the beginnin' of his idiotic per-

"The call Jim blew was the sweetest sound I ever heard."

formances that day, which cost us nearly half the troop.

"We crowded about halfway through the rocky pass, and there was no mass shootin' except from a scatterin' line on the rim-rock, a quarter of a mile away. That silence meant a lot to the sojers who'd fought Injuns before Ellis'd quit his nursin' bottle. All to onct there broke out from every side the wildest din of yellin' and screechin' that ever tortured mortal ears. Sioux lead came whizzin' down, and a smoke cloud hid everything a minute after, except the points of flame that shot from behind the rocks and trees in a complete circle around us. Five hundred Injun rifles was bangin' away and not a feathered head for us to aim at. Men was droppin' here and there, and more was hunched over their saddles, holdin' to the mane with both hands. Shot hosses began chargin' up and down, screamin' with fear and pain, while others went wild and started to mill. Round and round they went, buttin' and jammin', some fairly climbin' the others' backs. The troopers was waitin' for orders that didn't come. They tried to hold their animals, but it was no use. Inside of three minutes the whole command was a crazy, yellin', swearin' mob. We could 'a cut our way out if we'd got the orders, but Ellis, the rankin' officer, was gawkin' around like a scared half-wit. All the time sojers was goin' down like sheep in a hailstorm, without a chance to shoot back.

"Barker and me was caught in the mix together, and nearby was Second Looey Faversham, callin' the steadiest men by name, and beggin' them to straighten out. Then he yelled to Ellis to sound the charge for God's sake. But Ellis was speechless. His bugler'd been shot off his hoss and was close to us, a-hangin' to another feller's stirrup. Jim grabbed his trumpet, and Faversham saw him.

"'Quick, Barker, the charge!' he orders, and the call Jim blew was the sweetest sound I ever heard.

"At the first note the mounts began to scramble into line; in thirty seconds we made a front and was movin' forward toward open ground, drivin' the reds before us.

"ON A RIDGE ahead was a line of heavy firin'. We set out to reach it quick. Jim and me was amongst the leaders, him still buglin' away. In the middle of the excitement and danger Jim was thinkin' on'y of Thunder Bolt. He looked around for him, and there he was back in the rear with Ellis, the skunk, holdin' him in. The old black was rearin' and plungin' against the bit, for he knowed his place was in front. Barker aimed the horn backward and blew. Well, Thunder Bolt fairly jumped off the ground. A dozen men couldn't 'a held him then. He bolted through the crowd and raced up amongst the very foremost of the skirmishers. The lieutenant sawed on the reins, but it was no use, Thunder Bolt didn't even feel it. Jim could 'a riddled Ellis then and there, and no one been the wiser, for Winchester lead was flyin' everywhere. But he didn't. Ellis was yeller as Sioux ochre. Barker knowed and despised him; the whole command knowed and despised him.

"The braves kept runnin' back, shootin' quick and straight. Thunder Bolt had carried Ellis to the very front, and there the Injuns singled out his officer's uniform for a target. The next moment he wilted and slid out of the saddle. That instant Jim dashed for the big black hoss. If Ellis was dead, Thunder Bolt'd be Jim's again. But before Barker reached him the magnificent hoss was cut down, too. He plowed along on his knees toward Jim, then fell over kickin'.

"When we got to open ground and turned to face the redskins comin' up from the rear, there was honest-to-God tears streamin' down Jim's powder-smoked cheeks. The kid was heartbroken. Then the Sioux swept down and we had to shoot our hosses and lay behind 'em thirty hours, till help come.

"That was the Battle of Wounded Knee.

"Next day when the hostiles was drove off we went back across the fight ground. Ellis's body was riddled with a dozen bullets. The Injuns'd been at him and give him the dose a killed officer usually got. He was stripped and scalped . . . a green-feathered arrow stuck out of each eye-socket, and his heart waved on a sharpened limb of a nearby bush. Thunder Bolt was stretched out dead, not far away. Jim and me was standin' beside him while they was countin' the slugs in Ellis.

"'Old pal,' says Jim, 'I knowed he'd get his medicine some time and get it good—but I'm glad they've found one bullet hole less than there might 'a been.'"

COMING NEXT MONTH

THE FIRE-MASTER by SEABURY QUINN

A Moving Tale of the Spanish Occupation of the Low Countries.

Another Fine Thriller by H. BEDFORD-JONES

Have you a friend who will enjoy GOLDEN FLEECE?

If so, clip this coupon and we will send him a complimentary copy.

Name. . . . .

Address . . . .

(THIS OFFER EXPIRES FEBRUARY 1, 1939)

Tomorrow at Ten

by Robert Griffith

Illustrated by H. W. McCAULEY

CHAPTER I

SIR MAXWELL BLEY had put off his wig, and now he stood eyeing me. He was a shortish man, fat, with a swollen belly. His face was red and bilious looking; and I could not like his eyes, so cold and protruding and suspicious.

"You would, eh!" His fat lips curled

as he mocked me. "You—a down-at-the-heels dizzard from gad-knows-where, simpering at her heels scarce a month—and now, begad, you'd wed and wife her!"

"With your permission, sir," said I.

He laughed nastily, showing his great yellow teeth. "Damme! You have gall to purpose such a thing! Who the devil *are* you, anyway?"

I told him bluntly: "I am Dafydd Hughes, sir, of Llanuwchllyn. I am an honest man of good habit. I esteem your niece highly, sir, and she—"

"Your family?" he barked. "Your father—who?"

"My father was Captain Llewellyn Hughes. He was killed at Waterloo these two years agone, sir."

He was squinting at me, fingering the ruffle of his gold-figured waistcoat. "Humph . . . But you are not a soldier, eh?" He looked me up and down, and answered his own question: "No! Not with those yellow curls and the air of a country schoolboy. You have an income?"

"I have what I earn, sir."

He snorted. "That will be mean enough! What is your profession—milkmaid?"

I answered boldly (and it was only a half-lie): "I am a teacher, Sir Maxwell—"

"Ha! And why are you here in Horsham? There is no lack of teachers here."

I thought quickly. "I am a private tutor, sir. I had come up with my friend Cadwalader for a month's holidays in London; it was noisy there, and we—"

"Likely!" sneered he. "You had not come up from Llanu-what-the-devil-is-it with the idea of marrying for a bit of money, eh?"

BEFORE I could answer him this, he had turned abruptly and gone stamping from the room. I stood a moment, half minded to follow him and demand an apology, for his contempt had begun to nettle me. It was then, though, that I heard the rattle of some vehicle in the drive outside. There was a loud pounding at the door, and white-haired old Phineas, the butler, came running to open it.

A figure pushed hastily past Phineas; I saw his beaver and heard the coarse, familiar voice of Major Soares before I glimpsed his lean, cadaverous, grinning face.

"Hullo—hullo," he said to Phineas. "Sir Max about?"

I had backed to the wall; I felt a door behind me and I pulled it open to back into—a closet! But there I stayed; it would be most awkward to have Major Soares recognize me in this house.

Hiding thus in the dark, I heard Soares' greeting as Phineas fetched Sir Maxwell in. "How now, Maxel! Here I am, in a bloody hurry. You've got the rhino?"

Sir Maxwell said sharply: "Hold your tongue, fool! Miss Joyce is just outside with that pretty fellow—"

"He'll be out of the running shortly!" Soares' laugh was harsh.

Sir Maxwell was anxious. "Dirks has agreed?"

I pricked up my ears at that. Dirks? Would not that be Gentleman Jack Dirks, champion pugilist of England?

Soares answered: "Aye. The championship means little to brave Jack, when he may have so fresh a bride—and of the quality—for the losing of it."

Though these words perplexed me, they seemed to make Sir Maxwell well pleased. "Then it's settled?" said he eagerly. "Dirks will be beat by the Welshman—before the fifth round?"

"Aye," said Soares. "And as the Welshman's backer, I shall have your five thousand down—and a guinea or two for meself."

"Five thousand pounds!" crowed Sir Maxwell. "And bet at five to one! I shall pay off my debts! I'll have me stable again, begad, and—" But then he broke off suddenly. "Mind you, Soares, Dirks shall not have the troth

A sudden fit of rage came over me. I hardly restrained myself from bursting out upon them.

of Joyce till the fight is done. We'll have no double crosses!"

I was seized with a sudden chill as the gist of this talk came to me. It was incredible! Sir Maxwell Bley, baronet, supposedly wealthy—was he so impoverished and so base that he would sell the daughter of his blood brother to this brute of a Dirks?

Soares' voice was assuring. "Never fear, Sir Maxel. You well know how ambitious is this Dirks. What's the championship to him, when he may marry into the gentry? For that matter 'twill be a simple thing to get another match with the Welshman and regain his boxing honors. But first—the gentle wife!"

"Aye," sneered Sir Maxwell. "Though his father was a music hall buffoon, this Dirks affects the airs of a damned duke! But that's to our advantage."

They were walking down the hall; they stopped, and I heard a tapping, as of a boot against something solid. "There it is," came the voice of Sir Maxwell. "I'll have it put in your chaise. . . . And, damn you, have an eye out for thieves on the high road! This chest of gold is every cent I have to me name—and half of that borrowed."

I remembered then. Before Sir Maxwell had come from his study to talk with me, I had seen Phineas and a serving man carrying this heavy chest into the hallway. Five thousand pounds! And it was to be bet that the champion of England would be beaten! And he *would* be beaten—he would lie down; this great Dirks had sold his championship. And for his reward he would marry and have the pleasure of ravaging the woman I loved—innocent Joyce Bley!

A sudden fit of rage came over me. I hardly restrained myself from bursting out upon them. Yet, I forced myself to be calm. I waited, and when the two had gone into the study, I opened the closet and went on tip-toe to the big door and out of the house.

I WENT to the garden, where Joyce was waiting. She had been plucking some yellow jessamine blossoms for a bouquet, and now she rose from her knees, pushing the brown tresses from her brow. She must have sensed my failure, for there was a tragic look in her dark-lashed blue eyes.

"Dafydd—what has happened? You look so—so angry, Dafydd. Did Uncle say—?"

I sat down on the bench, eyeing my boots, trying to compose myself. "He told me I was a presumptuous ass—a penniless adventurer—and a bit more."

"Oh, Dafydd!" She was beside me, holding my hand, turning my face to hers. "Do not feel so bitter, Dafydd. Sometimes Uncle is a bit—choleric. Another time, Dafydd dear, when he has come to know you, it will be different. I know it will."

"Mayhap," I said, rather too cynically. In truth, it was not Sir Maxwell's rejection that so disturbed me, for I had anticipated that. But this other dastardly business had me raging and yet so confused that I knew not what to do or say. But I thought that I must keep it from Joyce. Yet, I did ask her: "Tell me this, Joyce: suppose your uncle were to choose a husband for you; would you feel bound to marry him?"

And she answered without hesitation, though her voice was low. "Yes, Dafydd, because it was my father's wish. . . . But," she added hastily, "my uncle would press no man upon me, Dafydd. And, after a little, when I have talked to him and persuaded him, he will give his blessing, and gladly. Oh! I am sure of that, Dafydd . . ."

Ah! thought I. How little you know the blackness of this uncle's heart, poor trusting Joyce.

We had sat in silence a moment, when my mare, Rhian, which I had left grazing outside the garden gate, came mincing up to nuzzle my shoulder. Joyce rose to stroke the mare's neck.

"Poor Rhian. She knows you're in trouble, Dafydd."

I said something; but all the time I had an eye on the drive, where it passed the garden. For the whirling puzzle that filled my mind one clear, quick, and sure solution occurred to me, and I made a decision to see it through.

Joyce was fondling the mare; her hand ran over the saddle and stopped at the big holster that hung there. She opened it and pulled the pistol half-way out. I saw her frown, and I knew what had caught her eye.

Aloud, she read the name graven on the silver plate at the pistol's butt—*Dave Savage*—, and she turned to me questioning.

"What an odd name . . ."

"An old friend," I told her. "The pistol was given to me for a keepsake."

I heard the wheels of a carriage in the gravel driveway and a stable-boy talking to his horses. There were the voices of Sir Maxwell and Major Soares from the big door. Then came Soares'

"Good even then, Sir Max!" and the carriage went past the gate, with the horses galloping. Two of Sir Maxwell's stable-hands rode with Soares, I noticed.

Now, I knew, I must act quickly. I went to Joyce, trying to smile and hide my excitement. I took her hands in mine. She came close to me, resting the brown head upon my shoulder, and I breathed perfume from the sprig of jessamine in her hair.

"You'll be coming back, Dafydd?"

"I don't . . . Of course. Tomorrow."

She let me go, and I swung into the saddle and galloped down the drive toward the high road without looking back at her.

THE sun had gone down and it was coming on fast to dusk. In another hour, I knew, it would be quite dark.

At the turn of the drive I saw the dust from Soares' chaise ahead, and I struck across into the lea and followed along the road's edge, always keeping that cloud of dust in sight. Thus for three or four miles, and then I cut across to the right. Straight this way for another two miles and I should strike the winding high road again.

The darkness had come when I reached it, and I dismounted to lead Rhian down into the shadow of a clump of young willows. There I took up my vigil, with ears strained to catch the first sounds of Soares' approach.

Perhaps twenty minutes had passed when I heard them. I leapt to the saddle and sat waiting in mid-road, watching the dim lights of Soares' lanthorn coming in the blackness.

When they were quite close, I spurred Rhian forward. We were at the horses' heads. I grabbed at their bits, twisting them savagely into the ditch. Then I was quickly by the carriage side, with my pistol levelled at the three within.

"Hands up—and out with you!" cried I (trying to disguise my voice). "One false move, and I'll blow your heads off!"

Soares cursed, trying to bring his horses about, but I reached over to yank the reins from his hands. I saw that one of the stable-hands had a blunderbuss, and I came closer, jabbing him sharply with the long pistol. "Drop it! Drop it! Out with you!"

The next instant the pistol was wrenched from my hand—the fellow had grabbed it from pure fright! He leapt to the ground and stood there atremble, clutching both blunderbuss and pistol.

"Begone wi' ye! Begone!" he quavered. " 'Gone—or I'll murther 'e—"

He was on the opposite side of the chaise, and I could do nothing but roar at him: "Drop that pistol! Drop it!"

The fool was so frightened he *did* drop it. But at that instant Soares jumped from the chaise; he was pawing for the pistol. I saw him bring it up; the noise of the discharge and the sudden flare of light startled Rhian. She reared up, almost unseating me.

The ball must have missed us, but then I saw that the other stable-man had a great horse-pistol; clutching it with both hands, he leveled it. And again came a thundering blast. Rhian screamed horribly, and I felt her sag under me. I thought she would flounder. Then she righted herself; but for all my strength on the bit, she reared again and wheeling, plunged madly down the black road. The roar of the blunderbuss followed us, and I heard the pellets rain against the leaves over my head.

The noise of the discharge and the sudden flare of light startled Rhian. She reared up, almost unseating me.

When I could pull up, I found reason enough for the mare's behaviour: a bloody ridge over her spine. There was here a rough road to the right, and I led Rhian away into the shadow. She quieted after a minute. While we waited there, Soares' carriage went careering by. One of the stable-men was lashing the horses madly, and the other I could see with his blunderbuss ready; and I knew that I must leave this business as a bad job.

CHAPTER II

IT WAS next afternoon that I went again to Bley House. And I went with some trepidation, I must confess.

Yesterday, wroth and confused, I had been too anxious to nip this plot of Sir Maxwell and Soares in the bud. Now, I thought of a dozen ways I might have employed—and successfully — to thwart them, without so prejudicing my honor. I cursed the foolhardiness that had sent me to the high road with a pistol.

But the mischief was done. And if my obliquity were discovered, I could only pray that Joyce show me charity and the hangman be sure with his rope. As I rode toward Bley House, I knew I was a fool to stay in England whilst I might yet escape. Yet, I had another task before me, and I was bound to finish it ere I fled. And then, here in England was Joyce . . .

I saw her walking beneath the great oaks of the drive, stopping now and again to look down the road; and I knew she was watching for me.

I had got a grey stallion from the village livery, and when I first dismounted, she asked why I had not brought Rhian. I told her the mare was being shod; though, in truth, it was the hole in Rhian's back that had made me leave her in her stall.

But then Joyce went into an excited (and a bit exaggerated!) account of the attempted robbery of Major Soares—and I trying to treat the subject jocosely.

"But Dafydd!" cried she. "A highway robbery, not five miles from this house!" And then: "You must be careful, Dafydd, not to ride the roads at night."

I said lightly: "I am far too poor for a highwayman's trouble."

Joyce took my arm and turned me toward the garden. "At least," she was laughing, "we need not fear the highwayman today," and she nodded toward the house. "My uncle has guests—the champion of England, no less!—and his trainer."

(Ah, thought I darkly, he has come to apprize his bargain!)

I HAD no fear of meeting these guests, for, except by name, I was unknown to any English sporting men. First, though, I hoped to have a minute alone with Joyce Bley; but I was disappointed in this. At the garden gate we encountered an odd person: a brightly dressed, weazened fellow, with a flattish face and sharp, squinting eyes. He doffed his hat elaborately to Joyce, and she presented him.

"Dafydd, you do not know Mr. Tom Traunt? He is the champion's trainer."

"I have heard most favourably of your man, Mr. Traunt," said I.

"Wot 'o," said Tom Traunt, without taking the hand I offered him. "Name o' Dirks is knowed w'ere the *h*art o' fightin's knowed, me lad."

He then turned his attention to Joyce, speaking with a familiarity that I thought unseemly, and ogling her the while.

"'Ave ye 'eard the latest 'bout this cove as was robbed, Miss Joyce? 'Twas none other than that bony devil Major Soares, the gambler—'im as is backin' the Welsher agin my big 'un for the championship."

"How strange," said Joyce.

I saw that the name of Soares was not known to her; and then I reflected: of course Sir Maxwell had kept secret the fact that he had dealings with the man.

"Ar!" Tom Traunt was saying. "They's more strange than that to the tale. Soares was a-carryin' a chest o' gold—five thousand pound 'e were to bet on 'is man—a-carryin' it to Bond

Street for the signin' o' *h*articles. —And 'oo does it turn out as robbed 'im—or tried to—but 'is own man—*the Welsher!*"

I found myself gaping at Traunt; and when his eye caught mine, I looked away in confusion, and I thought he noticed it. But Joyce, puzzled, was asking: "Why should this Welshman try to rob his own backer? That sounds silly!"

"W'y?" chortled Tom Traunt. "W'y indeed! 'Cause the bloody Welsher's afryd to step in the ring wi' Gentleman Jack the Chopper, that's w'y, me leddy! A-robbin' 'is own backer, so's 'e won't 'ave to fight my big 'un—y'see?"

Now I steadied myself and made another observation: Tom Traunt did not know that Dirks had sold out; this was a secret well guarded.

Joyce, woman-like, was asking: "And will they punish this Welsh fighter?"

"Ar!" said Tom Traunt, spitting through his teeth. "Punish 'im, ye say? —they'll 'ang 'im! Away to Tyburn Tree an' then gibbeted in irons on the King's 'ighway for the bloody robber 'e is. —That is," he added, "w'en they find the cove. Y'see there's none as knows 'is 'angout, 'im a-trainin' in secret like. But soon or late, they'll stretch 'is damned Welsh neck!"

"Oh—cruel!" cried Joyce. "And—how can they be sure 'twas he?"

"Ha!" Traunt grinned at her most offensively. "Didn't the cove run *h*off in such a desprit bustle 'e left 'is popps be'ind 'im!"

"Popps?"

"Ar—'is pistol. Two foot long it were, a-dec'rated wi' pure silver. An' Soares, not knowin' it were he's, 'anded it *h*over to the orf'cers. Ha! Did 'is *h*eyes pop w'en he sees the nyme wrote on the 'andle —Dyve Savage, *h*it says, for all the world to see—"

"Dave Savage!"

I knelt quickly and fell to cleaning my Hessians with a stick, not daring to look into her face as she pronounced that name.

"Ar!" Tom Traunt went on. "Dyve Savage—that be the Welsher's nyme, the bloody thief."

JUST then there was a shrill whistle from the house. Tom Traunt turned away quickly. "That'll be the big 'un," he said; and he clapped on his hat and hurried away.

Joyce stood stock still, her blue eyes dazed and hurt, fixed on my own. I could say nothing, and when she spoke finally, her voice was low and hesitant. "Dafydd . . . your pistol. It was your pistol . . ." And after a spell of silence: "Dafydd, yesterday, when you talked with my uncle . . . did he tell you that you must have money . . . to marry me?"

I saw tears shining in the pain of her eyes. I wanted to take her in my arms. Yet, I did nothing. And when I answered shortly: "He did imply that," my words sounded blunt and strange to me.

"And so," she stumbled on, "you went out . . . to *steal* money, Dafydd?"

That she should look upon it thus was a shock to me. I strove for words to deny the charge, but could only stand dumbly, praying that intuition would tell her that I had done this thing for love of her.

Her face was moved with anguish. And again she spoke dully: "And the pistol, Dafydd. You told me this person—Dave Savage—was your friend. Would you betray your friend, Dafydd, and see him hanged?"

I could only answer gracelessly: "I doubt he will hang." And all the time

I was trying wildly to find a way to tell her why I had done this, to tell her, and yet not wound her with knowledge of Sir Maxwell's perfidy.

Then she was leaning against the garden wall, her dark head bowed, sobbing brokenly. I went up to her; I held out my hand to touch her shoulder, and she moved quickly away, as if I would contaminate her.

"Oh, Dafydd!" she wailed. "You have been so foolish! Suppose you are discovered?" She lifted her face, and her eyes were wide with fear. "You will be hanged—*hanged,* Dafydd, for a thief! You who would marry me, who have been here in the house of Sir Maxwell—"

My temper broke, and I burst out wildly: "'Twould take more than a simple thief to dishonor the house of Sir Maxwell Bley!"

She stopped, staring at me. I saw her lovely face grow suddenly white. But I could not stop myself. "I had tried to spare you the pain of knowing your uncle for the wretch that he is!" I was shouting angrily. "And how he would shame you—he and that brute of a Dirks!"

She put her hands to her ears and started away, but I grasped her roughly and spun her about.

She turned on me then, struggling with more temper than I had reckoned for; and her face was flushed, her eyes blazing. "Coward!" she cried. "You would not handle this Dirks you malign so bravely, lest he box your tender ears!"

"Listen, wench!" I panted. "You will not so admire this fellow—when Sir Maxwell has made you his bride!"

I felt her relax all at once. I loosed her wrists, but she did not move; she only stared at me with eyes that held a shadow of fear. And I felt a sudden shame for myself and a pity for her.

"Joyce—Joyce!" I cried. "I did not mean to—"

But she was half raging, half crying: "Better to marry *him,*" she cried, "than a thief and a coward and a liar!"

"You would do better," I said hotly, "to save those words for a man they fit well—your blackguardly uncle!"

THERE were heavy footsteps in the gravel: I wheeled to see Sir Maxwell come puffing into the garden. His face was distorted with anger; he must have heard my loud charges, for he made straight for me. "Begone!" he raged. "Begone, sniveling scandalmonger—bullier of women! Get on your nag, sirrah, and leave! *Go!*"

I went up to him deliberately; and he changed, backing away with fright in his mottled face.

"Sir," I said. "I shall take the pleasure to slap your fat face before I go!"

But just then another figure loomed in the garden gate. I turned to face—instinctively I knew him—Gentleman Jack Dirks!

A moment we stared at each other. He was monstrous, a great, black-haired fellow. (I knew that he weighed well over sixteen stone!) His eyes, black and bright, set close together, sunk behind high cheek bones, were on me in a brute-like scowl. Drest like a dandy, the great breadth of his shoulders seemed all the greater for the tight-fitting scarlet spencer he wore. He was handsome in a bestial way, and there was about him a certain grace of movement and masterful air that gave credence to his reputation as a fighter.

But he eyed me only a moment, then, with a sneering laugh, he turned to Joyce and swung his fancy hat low in an exaggerated and practiced bow. I saw the black eyes go over her with such a look of lust as made my blood boil.

But then he turned, tossed his hat to the ground, took one step toward me. "Ah . . ." said he, in a voice I thought much affected; and he reached his hand toward me in a swift movement. "And you would slap Sir Maxwell's face, my pretty one—?"

"Or yours!" I snapped; and I knocked his arm violently down.

I saw murder leap to his eyes; his genteel pose was gone instantly. "Hey!" he cried out sharply. "'Ave a care, ye piddlin' young tippy!" He doubled one great hairy fist and thrust it under my nose. "Smell o' that afore ye get so 'igh and mighty wi' Jack Dirks!"

I pushed his fist away, and he flailed out suddenly with the other. I made him miss absurdly. He snarled and started another blow, but I held up my hand. "Save your wind, Dirks," I told him. "You'll need it shortly."

He stared at me in astonishment. Sir Maxwell's mouth hung agape.

"I had hoped to meet you a bit later," I said to Dirks, "in the ring at Dorking Downs. But, since I may save my neck by whipping you here and now—*let us at it!*"

He stepped back, staring at me. His voice was hoarse. "'Tis Savage!" he said in his throat. "Dave Savage!"

"Right," said I, stepping toward him with my guard up. "And now, if you will entertain me—"

"Coward!" she cried.

ERE my words had left my lips he was on me with a bull-like rush. I fibbed him cleanly between the eyes with my straight left, but I was borne back by the very power of his charge. He let go his right in a round-about swing, and I ducked it easily. But this only brought him to his senses. He stopped abruptly; he straightened, and up on his toes now, came into me with both hands held high.

I faced him confidently, sure of my game. His dark face was twisted in a ferocious scowl (to frighten me, I suppose); his great fists had begun to rotate, one about the other, and he was edging toward me. But I meant to show him speedily that I had no fear of him, and I stepped in smartly, feigning a fib to draw his punch—and he had walloped me thrice in the ribs ere I could spring back again! And swiftly he followed me, and twice smote me glancing blows along the jaw with a left that came like lightning!

Now I realized that the stories I had heard of this huge fellow were no wild tales. He was fast—faster than any man I ever had seen! And the power of his punches, though they had hit me in flight, was astonishing; my head was spinning, and my side felt as if a horse had kicked me there!

Yet, I would gamble my speed, if not my punch, against his, and again I darted in to fib him squarely on the mouth. But then something happened; I stepped back; my foot lagged in the soft ground. Dirks leapt in with the swiftness of a great cat; I felt the terrific force of his right fist bludgeon my jaw. I was rammed back against the stone wall. And ere I could get away, he had struck me again, and sent me floundering to the dirt.

I was badly stunned, but I put my feet under me and stood again. And when he lunged in, I grappled him and thrust him back. He was surprised at my strength; for an instant he was off balance, and I smashed him twice with wide right swings. I might have used a feather duster for all the effect my punches had. Dirks only tightened his grip of me; with his great weight he bore me back. And as I strained with all my power, he tripped me suddenly, hurled me to the ground and purred me squarely in the groin with his heavy boot.

I heard Joyce scream out. I heard Sir Maxwell's shrill words: "Well done, Dirks! Give him the boots again!"

But I had no taste for more of this foul business. I forced myself to my knees, and then I rose warily. My hands were down, clutching my belly, for I was so stricken with nausea I thought I should puke.

I backed away as Dirks charged me. Then he was upon me, his two fists slogging mercilessly. I could not see him; I tried to punch, but my arms were heavy. I thrust my head down and my arms out, trying to grapple him. . . .

CHAPTER III

NEXT thing I remember I was on my back. There was a soft hand caressing my brow and the smell of jessamine close to me. I sat up, bewildered to find Joyce kneeling beside me.

"Dafydd, speak to me . . ."

Her eyes were frightened. I could not find my tongue, but I nodded dumbly, and lay back again, for my head was awhirl.

"Oh! I thought you were dead, Dafydd . . ."

I lifted myself to one elbow and looked about. We were beneath one

"Oh! I thought you were dead, Dafydd . . ."

of the oaks by the drive. How I had got there, I do not know. Indeed, it was some minutes before the fight with Dirks came back to me. I sat up; my mind was confused; I could not think what had happened. Then, with my sore body, my jaws vibrating with sharp jumping pains, all the hazy remembrance that was left me came back, bit by bit. And I knew that Dirks had whipped me.

Joyce had brought my horse close by; now she tried to raise me from the ground. "Dafydd dear, you must flee! You haven't a minute to waste. Please, Dafydd—your life depends on it!"

I got to my feet giddily. "Madam," I said bitterly, "I am a Welshman; I shall not flee. Though the King's army try to stop me, I shall meet this Dirks again, and—" Then I stopped, knowing how vain my words must sound, when Dirks had thrashed me so easily. But to myself I swore I should some day have revenge for this beating.

Joyce was clinging to me. "Ah, you were brave, Dafydd, to fight him. But I will not let you in the brutal ring with so monstrous a man—'twould be murder! And then, did you not hear Tom Traunt's words? The officers will hunt you down; you will be arrested, Dafydd. 'Less you flee, you will be hanged!"

But in my mind was planted hate for Gentleman Jack Dirks, and a burning for vengeance that would not be appeased.

I looked down upon her soft cheek, wetted with tears. "I may be hanged," said I, "but if I be, I swear, it will be as champion of England that they gibbet me!"

Her face fell, but she importuned me no more, seeing that my mind was made up. Now, my giddiness was gone: I stood and walked about, my mind clearing. It came to me that I had given Joyce no explanation for my sally on the high road; she still had no knowledge of her uncle's foul design. And since things had come to this pass, I forthwith told her the whole tale.

Though my words shocked and wounded her, yet she would not doubt me. And I was gladdened to see how generously she put away her own sorrow and bent herself to aid me.

"Dafydd," said she resolutely, "you have done a noble deed. No English judge will see you punished for such a thing. We shall take this matter before some person of rank—"

"Ah, sweet Joyce," I said wryly, "what person of rank will help me, a Welshman—in England?"

"Many!" she cried quickly. "You are prejudiced against my people, Dafydd. I swear my uncle will aid you—"

I could not forbear a cynical laugh. But she stopped me.

"Not Sir Maxwell, but a bitter enemy of his: my mother's brother, Adam, Lord Birnie. And I shall see him at once! Tomorrow! Tomorrow I shall go to London . . ."

I had my arms about her slender shoulders. "Dear, noble Joyce, all the lords in the kingdom can not save a highway robber—"

"They can—they will! And my uncle Adam knows all the great ones at court, Dafydd. Oh, he will save you, Dafydd—I am sure of that!"

And her manner was so sure that I laughed aloud; and of a sudden there was great hope in my heart.

But now from the house came a loud hallooing: Sir Maxwell calling: "Joyce! Joyce!"

She embraced me quickly. But I

held her a moment. "Perhaps," I said, "it were better to feign that we are done with each other. And not to let Sir Maxwell know—what *we* know of his plans."

"That is my own thought," she whispered. And then, as she turned to go, she tossed me a sprig of jessamine from her hair. "Let this be our token. I shall send a messenger to you—day after tomorrow at the latest—and you will know him by such a sprig of jessamine . . ."

Then she was gone swiftly.

AND thus I rode down the road with a lighter heart than when I had come. For now I was sure that when this uncle of Joyce's had heard the story of Sir Maxwell's dastardy he would gain me a pardon. And he would see that I was given my chance to fight for the championship of England without fear that victory would be tainted with the corruption of Sir Maxwell Bley and Major Soares.

But as I rode along I realized suddenly that another horseman had been following at my heels all the way from Bley House. I had noticed the fellow but thought nothing of his presence. What made me wonder was that when I had galloped the first mile or so, he had matched my pace. And now that I walked the grey, he slowed up, keeping an even distance behind me.

To test my suspicion I spurred the grey to a gallop and held this pace till we had reached the Bell and Bottle Inn, and then pulled up sharply. And, sure enough, my horseman came on at a gallop too, till he spied me; and then he halted abruptly.

Thereafter I purposely ignored him. But I knew he kept me ever in sight, and this puzzled me. If I were to be arrested, why was it not done and got over? Why need this fellow linger?

It was thus wondering that I turned down the lane to the house where I lived with my trainer and friend, Owain Cadwalader. It was a great barn of a place, much out of repair. Yet, for its cheap rent and solitude, it had been ideal for our purpose.

I dismounted at the gate (the yard was surrounded by a great stone wall, some twenty feet in height) and led the grey down the drive, so long unused that the branches of bordering trees hung across it, blocking passage for a mounted man. When I had stabled the horse and come into the house, old Owain came running to me.

"Davey—Davey, ye've run off again and missed your hour with the mufflers," said he reproachfully. Little Owain came only to my shoulder; I looked down upon his bald head, into his bright blue eyes, worried now beneath their scarred brows. "This dalliance'll be the death of me, Davey *bach,*" he said. "And Major Soares, after his bringing you here from Wales and putting up money to back you, he wouldn't like it, Davey."

"Ah . . . would he not?"

"Nay. And your wench, lad, doesn't she know a fighting man has training to do, and all of us worrying—"

"You need worry no longer," I told him shortly, making to leave the room.

Owain brightened at that; but then he eyed me anxiously. "But Davey, ye have the look of a man with the *cryd*—art ill, boy? Or ye've had trouble with the lass, mayhap?"

I shrugged my shoulders and started away, but the old fellow caught my sleeve. "Tell old Owain, lad," he begged. "What is it—has she sent ye away—because ye're a prize-fighter?"

"I told her I was a teacher—I did not say of boxing."

He was hurt at that, and stood there shaking his head. "Dave Savage, champion of Wales—are ye ashamed of the honor ye've won in the ring, lad?"

I told him bitterly: "I admit my mistake. I had thought that a prize-fighter would be unwelcome in the house of the Bleys. Now I have found that greater villains than I come there—but none so great as Sir Maxwell himself!"

For an instant I considered telling Owain the whole story; but I decided against it, for I well knew his distrust of the English. He would have demanded that we leave England forthwith.

I HAD just turned to go upstairs, when there was a great pounding at the door. I went to the window and espied three men at the threshold. Burly fellows they were, dressed much alike, each with a bright red waistcoat. And stranger though I was in England, I sensed that these were officers.

I grabbed up a pistol from the mantleshelf and walked toward the door, hardly knowing what I was about.

Old Owain stopped me. "Are ye daft, Davey? What is it ye fear that ye'll need a pistol to answer a knock at the door?"

I put the pistol down reluctantly. It hurt me to see the bewilderment in Owain's battered face. I started again for the door, but he stopped me.

"Wait. Let me greet . . . our visitors."

And so he went to the door; and from the window I watched him come out to face the three strangers. He addressed them with a courteous salute: "What would you have, good friends?"

The largest of them stepped up to Owain. "We'll 'ave a chat wi' you, old cove," said he. "Could ye tell us now, the whereabouts of one Dyve Savage?"

"Davey?" said old Owain. "Why I'm expecting the lad momently. What would ye be wanting of my Davey, friends?"

"We'd be wantin'," said the fellow, "to do a bit o' lookin' about wiles yer Davey's away." And he thrust himself past Owain and started through the door.

"Hold, friend!" cried Owain; and I saw him grab the fellow's arm and set him on his gammons with a dextrous twist. The other two jumped forward, but there was something in the calm, scarred face of Owain that made them hesitate.

The fallen man scrambled up. " 'Ere now!" he brayed. "Hi'll learn ye the way to treat orf'cers o' Bow Street court!" And he fetched out his pistol, beckoning his mates toward the door. "In wi' ye, chaps, wiles I covers the old cove."

Owain Cadwalader spread his arms wide, barring the way. "Barkers or

Sure enough, my horseman came on at a gallop, till he spied me; then he halted abruptly.

no," he said calmly, "I'll have the three of you on your buttocks in the dirt, if ye make a move to enter this house!"

"Arter 'im!" cried the big fellow.

I was about to run to Owain's aid, when there came another voice, hard and coarse, from the lane. "Stop! What the devil's the meaning of this?"

I knew that voice, and I peered out to see Major Soares walking toward the house, his horse following behind. It was plain, too, that these three knew the Major, for they bobbed their heads and stood waiting uneasily as he came up.

The big one mumbled: "We're a-makin' a 'vestergation, yer honor, sir."

Soares stood glaring at the man, with his arms akimbo, and his bony, villainous face screwed up in a fierce scowl. But first he spoke to Owain.

"Stable my horse, Cadwalader. I'll be rid of these blundering bum-bailiffs shortly."

HE waited till Owain had gone with the horse, and then he began to berate the three men hotly. "Investigation, you say? Ha! Prying poltroons, Lord Howard shall hear of this! Have you not his orders to see that the Welshman does not escape—but to keep your prodding noses out of the affair? Investigation indeed! 'Tis petty thievery you're up to, I'll venture—"

"But, yer honor—'twill take everdence to 'ang the chap, sir—"

"Dunderhead! We have evidence enough to hang him a dozen times! Yet, the Welshman is to be spared till he has fought Jack Dirks, d'ye understand? You blunderers — would you frighten him away?"

"Never fear," said the burly one. " 'E'll ne'er get away, yer honor. There be six of us; if 'e try an' skip, 'e's a dead 'un! An' we ain't a-lettin' 'im out o' our sights, yer honor sir—"

"Fumblers! Cabbage-heads!" snarled Major Soares. "See that you keep out of *his* sight! Now—away! Begone!"

They slunk away into the wood at his command. As for me, I began to see that my trouble was deeper than I had supposed. The name of this Lord Howard meant nothing to me; but it had had its effect on the officers. It was plain that this scheme of Sir Maxwell's had support from high places. And now I wondered if this uncle of Joyce's might not find it impossible to aid me, after all.

Yet I was relieved in some measure. At least, I should not be arrested till I had fought Dirks—and that gave me three weeks dubious grace.

I saw that Major Soares was coming into the house; but just then came old Owain back from the stables, and Soares turned to greet him. Now the scowl had left the Major's face, and in its stead was the malevolent grimace that was his smile.

"I have news for you, good Cadwalader," said he. "And good news, too."

Cadwalader looked doubtful. "What might it be, sir?"

"You know there's been a move afoot to stop our fight? It had begun to look as if these damned reformers would have some success—so the fight will be held ere any can stop it: tomorrow morn at ten!"

"It cannot!" said Owain sharply. "My man is not ready—"

"Ready enow, good Cadwalader," grinned Soares. "—And far readier than the champion. It is a point in our favour."

I felt my breathing quicken. Tomorrow morn at ten. There could be no help from Joyce nor Lord Birnie now. There could be no foiling of Sir Maxwell's plan now, unless it were flight; and I could not bring myself to consider that. With black dejection in my heart I faced the morrow.

Then should I step through the ropes to face monstrous Gentleman Jack Dirks the Chopper, a mummer in this travesty of battle for a dishonoured title? And should I go through the burlesque of knocking Dirks out to make it possible for him to marry the woman I loved?

And should I, Dafydd Hughes, called Dave Savage, having become Champion of England, let myself be led to the gallows and hanged for a highwayman . . .?

OWAIN roused me from a troubled sleep at five o'clock next morning, and I went down to breakfast. Major Soares was at the board before me. He looked up with his villainous grin and saluted me: "Good morrow, Dave Savage—champion of England!"

I should have taken pleasure then to slap that leering, cadaverous face; but I had my part to play, even as he played his, and I returned the greeting civilly.

Owain had prepared a great beef steak for my breakfast; I had no appetite, yet I stuffed it down rather than worry him more. I knew that my strange actions of yesterday had given him a sleepless night.

Now, in the clearness that comes with morning, I put the facts of my problem before me; and suddenly there came to me a glimmer of hope and a plan that might yet save Joyce from her uncle's machinations. Sir Maxwell's wager was that I should knock out Dirks before the fifth, that is, in one of the first four rounds. But, before Dirks could be knocked out, he first must be struck. And, reasoned I, if I strike him not, how may he fulfill his base bargain?

And so that was my plan. I must let him beat me for the first four rounds; I must not strike him, or give him reason to feign a knockout. Yet, in so doing, I knew I ran the risk of being knocked out myself. And the greater danger: that the Umpire, seeing me refuse to strike Dirks, might stop the bout and send me from the ring branded a crosser.

And as for my hanging, no sooner was breakfast done than I got my double-barreled pistol and put it in the bag that held my boxing paraphernalia. Dead men do not hang. And while there was life in my body Bow Street would have to fight for it.

Everything had been made ready, and half-an-hour after breakfast we set out for Dorking Downs, in Surrey, where the fight was to take place. The three of us went together: Owain, Major Soares, and myself, in a brougham that had been sent down from the village.

Before we had come to the village, I heard the sounds of horses' hooves, and turned to see three men (who could be none other than the officers) galloping not a hundred yards behind.

It was a sultry morning, with a threat of rain; but as we drove rapidly along, the sun came peeping out, and such hopes as I had harboured for postponement vanished.

Over and over in my mind I fought the battle that was to come, fought carefully the one way that might foil the plot of my enemies. I tried to sleep, but always there was the coarse, harsh voice of Major Soares in my ears and his staring eyes on me with a sardonic inner amusement.

Owain sat next the window, with his hands folded patiently. "They'll be praying for ye back in Wales this day, Davey *bach*," he said once. "And ye will not fail them. But mind this, lad: we've trained ye for a short go; Dirks outweighs ye three stone and more, and your best hope is your punch and your quickness. Ye've got to get atop your man quick and hammer him hard where it hurts—and then away till ye have another chance. Just as ye whipped Hew a Gwehydd, at Eglwysig. Mind ye, keep fibbing and shifting, no matter how the Fancy may hoot and howl . . ."

(Aye, thought I, they will hoot and howl, Owain!)

"Shift and fib, lad," Owain droned on. "Shift and fib, and keep your feet ever moving . . . and there'll be bonfires in the hills of Cymry this night . . ."

WE HAD ridden two hours before we turned off the road into a rutted by-lane; then I knew we were at the chosen place, for now on both sides were all fashions of vehicles and growing thicker as we advanced. It put me in mind of the Fair at Machynlleth.

Our brougham stopped. Owain was getting out. He beckoned me to follow, and when I did, a great crowd of men came rushing up, and they stood jostling and staring at me as if I were some unnatural monstrosity in a booth. Owain hustled me through the crowd and into a tumbledown pavilion that stood at the edge of a scraggy wood.

Even as I followed Owain into a small room within, I heard the loud voice of Dirks across the hallway, cursing with such venom as startled me, though I had seen him raging in the garden at Bley House. "Fetch me breeches, ye—lout!" he was ranting (to one of his attendants, I guessed). "Quick — Quick! — or I'll slit your damned throat! And 'ere! Clear the blasted crowd! Out! Out, damn ye!"

I wondered now if Dirks was regretting his bargain, for it surely sounded so. But this could not affect my plan. The bet was made, and whether he went down from my blow or in accordance with Sir Maxwell's scheme, Joyce would be his. And so, for four rounds, come what might, I must not strike him once.

For an hour there was a great coming and going, a constant buzzing of conversation, the slamming of doors, and rattling of arriving carriages. And all the time I could hear the bettors: "Two to one on Dirks," and then, when it was near ten o'clock, I heard them offering as high as sixty and seventy pounds to ten that I should be whipped. But there was little money bet on my chances.

After awhile a fellow in the blue and yellow uniform of the Pugilistic Club came in to enquire our choice of officers. Owain told him that we should have Soares as Arbitrator, and himself as second. A chowder-headed youth named Pillon was my Bottle-Holder; and Owain agreed on one Abner Coleman for Umpire. Then the uniformed fellow made certain that I knew the Broughton Rules: " . . . that when a man falls, the round shall be ended . . . if a Second does not bring his man to scratch within the space of half a minute, he shall be deemed a beaten man . . . that such disputes as the Arbitrators cannot settle the Umpire shall decide . . . that no man hit his adversary when he is down, or seize him by the ham, the breeches, or any part below the waist . . .", and so forth.

Whereupon, he wished me luck and went his way.

At quarter past ten we heard the crowd hurrying from the pavilion, and then the sounds of Dirks and his party leaving their room. Then there came a tremendous roar, such as I had never heard before, and I knew Dirks had come into the ring.

Owain had gone out of the room; now he returned, and nodding wordlessly, lifted me from the bench. He was tense and his eye sick with worry.

He said: "All right, Davey *bach,*" and tried to smile. We went out of the pavilion, with Soares and the Bottle-Holder following after.

A great drumming of feet and chatter of voices came to us as we neared the place; and on turning out of the wood into full view of the crowd I had to stop a moment, overcome by the sight of this multitude. The arena was a natural theatre in a deep cup of the downs; shoulder to shoulder they sat, fully five thousand persons. Owain pulled me forward gently.

"Steady, Davey."

Major Soares (he had a finger in the promotion) muttered: "The Door-Money'll bring a pretty penny . . . at half-guinea a head."

We went down the hill, and as the crowd spied us there came a spattering of handclaps. Here and there in the crowd I heard a few voices in Welsh: my own people wishing me courage. But for the most part the crowd merely stared at me.

BY THE time we had come into the ring a great stillness hung over them. I was covered with a large red robe. As I stepped through the ropes I started over to offer Dirks my hand. He looked up, scowling, and then away quickly, so I stopped and turned back to my own corner.

The sun was behind the clouds, which hung heavily now. Old Owain tied to the ring-post my scarf—my colors: a red dragon on a field of black, with the green Welsh leek in one corner.

Now the officials talked endlessly in mid-ring. The crowd was clamouring for the fight to begin. A blue-coated man introduced to me as *Commissary of the Fancy* came to my corner to examine my hands and person. He went back to talk with the others, and there was more howling from the crowd.

I saw the scarlet waistcoats of the Bow Street runners; they crouched at ring side, waiting like birds of carrion, to claim me for the gallows when the fight was done.

Then the Umpire cleared the ring. A man with a great bellows of a chest was holding up his hands for silence; and though he got only more noise, he bawled out the names and weights heroically, and then retired from the ring.

The Time keeper came round to my corner and asked if we were ready—

CHAPTER IV

I SAW Dirks stand and throw off his greatcoat, and a noisy burst of cheering swept over the multitude. I could only stare at the magnificent dark body of this famed champion of England, naked, save for the scarlet knee breeches of China silk, held with a broad white and blue ribband about his waist. It was more like the sculpture of some ancient master than any human I ever had seen.

A feeling of dejection came over me; but at Owain's command, I doffed my robe, and stood waiting in the corner.

I looked again at Dirks. His dark face was sullen. He turned about and stood looking out over the crowd belligerently, wetting his lips. This was a bold deed that he had before him, to dishonor the championship of England before this intense and excited crowd. I could see that he had little taste for it. Yet, I knew that for this prize—the troth of Joyce Bley—he had the brute lust and courage to risk his life.

I drew a deep breath and stepped a pace from the corner. A strange tightness came upon me. I thought of lovely Joyce Bley to give me courage for what I was about to do. The voice of the crowd had lowered to a surging, moving whisper. The Timekeeper lifted his right hand slowly, eyes upon his watch—

"Time!"

I walked out slowly to scratch. The crowd was suddenly still. I heard old Owain's voice, broken with quick alarm: "Fast, Davey! *Fast!*"

But I stopped at the mark and stood looking up at Dirks. His face was working; there was rage smouldering in his black eyes. His guard was well up in the pose for which he was famed. I stood erect, with my hands at my sides.

"Come, you great hulk of a pig!" I sneered. "Come closer, that I may bounce you on your fat buttocks!"

The black rage surged over him; instinctively his head went down and his right whipped, club-like, in a violent round-about punch. I stepped in carefully and came up on my toes to catch the blow glancingly on my shoulder—and threw myself to the turf as though the punch had knocked me down.

Even before I landed, a great howl of protest burst from the crowd—

"Coward! Quitter!"

"Stand and fight like a man, Welsher!"

I made a play of struggling to my feet. I had just risen, when there was a pounding of feet on the turf, and Dirks was upon me! He had slogged me twice foully before his Second and the Umpire caught him. They were in mid-ring shouting wildly, trying to hold Dirks.

The Umpire had him by the right arm, yelling: "Back to the corner, sir! Back!"

But still Dirks struggled, cursing wildly, so enraged that he would continue despite the rule that the round had ended when I went down.

Then there was another figure in the ring: Sir Maxwell Bley! His red face was distorted with panic; he was screaming: "Dirks! Dirks! *Dirks!*"

Owain came quickly to bring me back to the corner, and there was stark tragedy in his old eyes. "Davey—Davey," he was muttering hoarsely; "ye were not hit hard enow to go down, Davey *bach*. Why did ye do it, lad?"

"Leave me be, Owain," said I. "I know what I'm about."

While I waited the half-minute rest, I watched the other corner. Sir Maxwell had his face down next Dirks; he was pleading excitedly, oblivious of the crowd. The Umpire came to order him from the ring.

WHEN we came to scratch for the second round I was disheartened to observe that Dirks' anger had left him. He was even grinning maliciously; and he came to meet me with his hands down. He stuck his chin out invitingly.

"Here, my pretty Welsher! I'll give

'e a plain target. Hit it!"

I only stood regarding him silently; but he egged me on: "Come, little tumbler—I promise I'll not strike thee till ye've took thy best poke at my chin. *Hit it!*"

Whereupon there came a great roar of laughter from the crowd. But two could play at this game. With arms akimbo I regarded him a moment; then I stepped up to him deliberately—and spat in his face!

He grabbed me, cursing hotly. I felt his great arms about my neck in a chancery hold. He lifted me, flung me wide. And I, suddenly relinquishing my hold, dropped again to the turf.

And now the howls of the crowd held a threat of riot—

"Up, Jerry Sneak! Do ye fight on yer gammons?"

"Umpire! Umpire! D'yer know a cross w'en yer sees one?"

I scrambled to my feet, and looked about the ground with mock anger, as if I would blame my fall on faulty turf. But this did not deceive them. The thunder of howls rained down on me with increasing fury.

The Umpire strode after me to the corner. "'Ere, damn yer carcass, Savage!" he blustered. "Wot fashion o' boxin' d'yer call this? I gi' ye warnin', sir—'it the grass again wi'out bein' struck, an' the purse'll go to Jack Dirks!"

I said nothing. Owain was beside me, his lips trembling, and his voice near to crying. "Davey, Davey—have ye lost courage, boy? Can't ye hear the Saxons taunting ye? Davey—if ye go down, go down *fighting!* What will they say in Llanuwchllyn? Would ye shame the Welsh that love ye, Davey *bach?*"

I was in no mood for this scolding and I said sharply: "Hold your tongue, Owain—and bedamned to the Umpire and the Saxons and all of them! I have more on my hands than you know."

And old Owain's mouth clamped shut; but the pain in his eyes cut me to the heart. Before I could say more, however, time was called for the third round, and to the tune of loud jeers from the people, I walked out slowly again to scratch.

To myself I was saying: two rounds gone, and two to go—and then I may fight! But the voice of the crowd had lowered to a growling mutter that boded ill for me, and I knew I was in a quandary indeed.

DIRKS had changed. He came from his corner in a headlong rush, and was upon me ere I reached the mark, fibbing like lightning with his left. Twice it smote me full in the face. I was jolted back onto my heels before I could get out of range.

And Dirks was snarling: "Fight, Welsher! Fight! *Fight!*"

I was taken unawares; yet I stuck to my plan. Though I was sorely tempted to let go a blow with all my strength full between those brutish eyes, I held my temper, backing before his charge, with my head bobbing and ducking.

The great crowd was shrilling with wild excitement, yelling madly, urging Dirks to the knockout they thought was near. But I kept backing and turning and twisting, never once trying to hit; and suddenly the cheering dropped off, and a thousand angry voices were cursing and jeering me.

And still Dirks rushed in with his two fists swinging; and still I ducked and dodged and shifted, so that, save for the first two or three, none of his blows struck me squarely. But then one of them did; by an awkward twist when I was penned in a corner, I ducked full into one of them; and I was quickly undeceived as to Dirks' intention. These blows looked dangerous to the crowd, but they carried no power. Jack Dirks had no intention of damaging me; he wanted only to force me to mill, to give him a reason to go down and have an end to this burlesque.

But when he saw that I would not mix with him, he stopped the pursuit suddenly and turned to the screaming mob, signalling his disgust in elaborate pantomine and bellowing: "I come 'ere to fight, not to run a bloody race—and bedamned if I'll chase the yellow-bellied Welsher another bloody foot!"

The crowd cheered him lustily for that speech—

"Well said, brave Jack!"

"Hey, Umpire — make the Welsh coward fight or quit the ring!"

"Where's your bloody bottom now, Welsher?"

I saw now that I was undone unless I could rouse Dirks' anger and make him keep punching, and I made one desperate bid.

"Come, come, my handsome pantaloon!" I taunted him. "Can't you make a better play at fighting than that? This is but piddling business—for the son of a music hall buffoon!"

I saw him start, and murder lit his black eyes, for to his snobbish ambition, his father's humble trade was a thing of shame.

And again he was plunging across the ring with the charge of a madded bull. But this time I could not evade him, for I knew the crowd's temper was near breaking. I must stand to Dirks and take my punishment though I dare not hit him. I must take my fill of his blows before I went down, else the crowd would rush the ring to wreak their vengeance on me and all would be lost.

But even as I walked full into him with my hands belly high, ready to take his blows, I caught the smirk of cunning on his face. He swung a terrible round punch for my head—and missed by half a foot. He swung again and missed, and this time left himself clumsily open for a counter.

But I was ready, and as awkwardly as he, I heaved the counter wide of its mark, and sent another blow flying that missed as badly.

NOW the voice of the enraged mob was a single threatening monstrous howl. There was danger rampant, and when Dirks' next punch slapped harmlessly into my back, the Umpire jumped suddenly between us.

"Hold! Hold!" he barked. "Enough! This fight is too foul to go on!"

And even as he spoke a score of roughs had rushed the ring. And the "whippers in," whose duty is to quell such riots, were wielding their truncheons freely. And now the few roughs were joined by others; the "whippers in" were being driven back to the ropes.

Major Soares and the other Arbitrator were arguing angrily with the Umpire the while; and I went back to my corner with white-faced old Owain at my side. And as I stood there gazing out at the howling, madded crowd, I picked out a group of men coming toward the ring: a huge man in a great coat and plumed hat, and with him a white-haired man, a boy in a topper, and one or two others. Then the men at the ring side were between us and I lost sight of them.

The Umpire stood in mid-ring, both his hands waving frenziedly. "No bets to be paid!" he was screaming. "No bets to be paid! No bets—"

And at that instant I got a terrible blow on the head from behind. Strong hands grabbed me and bore me to the ground. I struggled to my knees, striking out wildly, but again I was felled with a thwack on the head. I scrambled away on all fours; I rose, and then I caught a flash of color, a scarlet waistcoat—the Bow Street officers!

I plunged across the ring, forgetful of the double-barreled pistol that was in my robe behind the ring-post. If there was a way of getting through this angry mob, I should chance it. But ere I had reached the ropes, another huge figure was before me; great arms closed about my middle, bore me to the ground! I lifted both myself and him from the turf, but still another hurled himself upon us, and I was thrown and pinned to the turf. I struggled frantically. Then I felt a band of steel close on my right wrist, and another on my left. I was yanked roughly to my feet, and found myself manacled by heavy darbies to a burly officer on either side, and three or four others were close about with cocked pistols in their hands.

A moment the officers and I huddled there; they were somewhat reluctant to take me out of the ring. I saw that the "whippers in" were fighting a losing battle with the mob. Already a dozen had broken into the ring and were engaged with the Seconds and other officers.

But then of a sudden there was a roaring, snarling voice, breaking through above the clamour. "Out of my way, blackguards! Out of my way or I'll have your heads, damn you!" And a huge, muffled figure, the same I had noted in the crowd a moment before, standing head and shoulders above the others, came plunging through the mob to vault the ropes. And beside him and around him were other men, half a dozen of them, each with half-drawn sword or pistol ready.

And this fellow did not stop at the Bow Street men but came cuffing his blundering way through, scattering them like nine-pins, to halt before me.

CHAPTER V

HE WAS a huge man, most of his figure hidden by the great, rich looking coat of fur. But it was his face, half shadowed by a plumed hat, that held my eye. An arrogant, overbearing face, it was, with a wisp of moustache beneath its purple veined and shapeless swelling of a nose. The eyes were cruel, leering from a face that was pimpled and pock-marked and bloated.

"So!" yawled this fellow, squinting one evil eye. "So—this pretty beggar calls himself—*champion?*"

Whilst he stood before me, I noticed that the voice of the mob had dwindled suddenly, and I knew that this man's loud and authoritative presence had stayed, for the minute, their crazed design.

But now this strange fellow thrust his foul face close to mine. His thick, flabby lips were twisted in a loathsome snarl. "Dog!" he bellowed in my face. "Craven! Dunghill cock! Is this what they call fighting in Wales?"

And then he slapped me heavily, full across the cheek.

I forgot the irons in my temper and made to strike back, but all I did was to wrench forward the officer to whom my right was manacled.

One of the Bow Street runners was protesting to the big man. " 'Ere now, yer honor, me lord, sir—we claims this man in the name o' 'is Majesty, the King—"

"The King?" snarled the pimpled man. "The King?—*Damn the King!*"

And while the officers stood aghast at this infamy, Major Soares came shoving his thinness forward. "Here, damn you rogues! What the devil's about? You can't arrest this fellow till the fight's done! I'll have you lashed, you—" And then his words stopped in his throat, for he had spied the fur-coated man. His bony face twitched and paled, and he snatched off his hat and made a hasty leg. "Your Highness—!"

And, staring, the officers hastily followed his example. But I could only gape and wonder. A sneering grin played now on the lips of the big man. His tone was quieter when he asked the officer: "On what charge do you claim this rascal?"

" 'Ighness . . . two days agone 'e 'eld *h*up 'is own backer on the 'igh road near 'Orsham . . . a-'opin' to get out o' fightin' Jack Dirks by thievin' 'is own backer's money, 'Ighness . . ."

Old Owain was at my side. "Tell them, Davey!" he cried. "Tell them ye're no *lleidyr,* Davey!"

The evil eyes turned to me. "Is this charge true, Welshman?"

I spoke out boldly: " 'Tis true—but for damned good reason, sire!"

"Ha! And what good reason, Welshman?"

"Because," I said, "I found that my backer was in league with Sir Max Bley—they had bought out Dirks—he was to feign a knockout—his price, the hand of Sir Maxwell's niece! I tried to stop Soares—and they call it robbery! And in this fight I dare not hit Dirks or give him reason to go down—"

Sir Maxwell was blatting loudly: "A lie! A base lie!"

The pimpled man blasted Sir Maxwell with a thundering *"Silence!"* And then he grinned maliciously in the baronet's mottled face. "The Welshman's tale fits you well, fat Max!"

Sir Maxwell could only gulp and stutter and back away. But now Jack Dirks from behind was thrusting himself forward. He alone, of all of us, was bigger and taller, and he called out boldly: "Wot's all this tarradiddle? 'Oo says as Jack Dirks'd fight a cross? I was but playin' wi' 'im! I'd broke the sneak's back wi' a blow, if he'd stand an' fight!"

Sir Maxwell was pulling violently at Dirks' arm, but the champion went on ranting as he pushed up behind the pimpled man. But then, at sight of the fellow's face, Dirks blanched; he turned about abruptly, and hid himself in the crowd that filled the ring.

HERE I broke in boldly: "Sire, I've spoke the truth. But if the Umpire will call 'all bets off' officially, then, by your leave—whoever you be—let the fight go on. And I promise you, I shall give this Dirks his belly full of Welsh fighting!"

The man was staring at me, and then a weird grin moved his ugly face. He nodded, as if most pleased. "Good. Good, Welshman."

He turned to one of his attendants (who only now sheathed the sword he had held ready). "See that the Welshman is loosed. We shall see some blood

And with my shoulder behind it, I let go my own right . . .

spilt yet, I promise you!" And then: "Fetch Dirks to me."

Dirks was brought reluctantly forward, his black eyes shifting uncertainly. " 'Ighness," said he, knuckling his forehead, "I swear by the cross there's no word o' truth in this Welsh liar's story—"

A mighty grunt and the pimpled man thwacked his open palm across Dirks' face with an equally mighty curse. "Hear me, trickster!" bellowed he. "You shall prove him a liar with your two fists—and you shall beat him unmercifully, else you leave this place in irons!"

"And *you!*" He wheeled to glare at me. "You, my yellow curls; I give you this choice: whip Jack Dirks and ye go back to Wales a free man. But if ye be beat—*then ye hang!*"

He turned abruptly to leave the ring by my corner. But when he went past me, he stopped, as if on afterthought, and reaching down, pressed something soft into my palm. And I was gaping—for the eyes that had gleamed with such arrant ill-humor held now a look of ironic amusement!—and the right eye drooped briefly. Was that not a sly wink?

I stared at the object that had been thrust into my hand. A blossom! A yellow blossom—a sprig of jessamine! From Joyce—her messenger!

I gasped in the Umpire's ear: "Who *is* this fellow whom all obey so fearfully?"

He eyed me askance. "You do not know George Augustus, boy?"

The Prince Regent!

George Augustus, Prince of Wales! Somehow, at the petition of Joyce or her uncle, Lord Birnie, the prince had come in the nick of time to save me from arrest and dishonor!

And now I saw a reason for all his thundering!—by this play of snarl and bombast, the masterful stroke of a showman, he had got respect from this dangerous mob; he had calmed the riot just before it was entirely out of hand!

But now the ring was cleared again; the crowd was waiting in muttering tenseness. The Timekeeper's voice came clear and loud—

"Time!"

Owain sent me from the corner with a mighty shove. Dirks was at scratch before me, and before I was in range he had hurled his famed chopping right-hander. But I had an eye on his chin; I was anxious to show this mob that I could mill. And with my shoulder behind it, I let go my own right—

THEN suddenly it seemed as if the heavens had fallen! Again there were the horrible noises of the thousands. But they faded abruptly and all was blackness and flashing before my eyes. I strove madly to punch—and drove my fists down into the turf, for I was lying on my face. I was down . . .

Owain's arms were about me; he was dragging me, and though I tried to put my legs under me, they were as legs of water. I had the feeling that I was falling, falling into some bottomless pit. All the noises faded then, and I was left weak and tired.

I could not stand. But I felt myself being lifted, lifted over the ropes. The fight was done—I had lost! But no—when I forced my eyes open, I was being lifted *into* the ring! Dirks must have knocked me completely over the ropes!

Then there was a spell of blankness, with only the sensation of thudding, pain-laden blows all over me, blows that I could not dodge because I could not see them. And there was the taste of blood and grass and brandy in my mouth and the smell of sweat and smelling salts in my nose.

The next thing I knew I was standing with legs wide apart, bewildered, staring out over the wildly screaming, gesticulating crowd that went whirling about me in a crazy, lop-sided circle. I looked to the unsteady ground beneath me. Writhing there I recognized the form of Gentleman Jack Dirks!

Old Owain was tugging at my arm. "Davey—to your corner!"

I followed him then, barely able to stand or to see. I stumbled and fell headlong into the ropes and then tumbled to my haunches and stayed there. I felt the hardness of a bottle thrust between my teeth, and I gulped, half choking, a great draught of hot brandy.

"'Tis the thirty-ninth round," came Owain's voice through the mist of my mind. "If ye can save your strength another five rounds, lad, and catch him again with that right-hander—"

"Owain—Owain!" I cried out, and I found myself laughing giddily. "Owain, man, you're out of your head! 'Tis but the fifth round—"

Owain tilted me head back of a sudden and looked into my eyes in what seemed to be alarm. "Ecod!" said he. "It's you, Davey, that's been out of your head these thirty-odd rounds! And I never knew it, for ye've been fightin' so like a lion!"

I had the feeling that I had just awakened, and with it came biting pain in every part of my body. I put my hand to my eye to see what made things to appear so oddly; my right eye was closed entirely, and the left was naught but a slit. There was the sting of skinned flesh on my face; I looked down at my arms and belly and found them torn and bruised.

I looked, squinting through my one eye, across the ring to the huddle of men about Jack Dirks' corner. Just then came the voice of the Timekeeper. The men about Dirks' corner stood up, and I saw his Second lean down and sink his teeth into Dirks' ear!

Owain had seen it too, and he said to me quickly: "This is the round, Davey *bach!* You saw them at the ear to bring him around? Dirks is worse hurt than I thought. Up on your feet, boy. This is the round!"

Owain lifted me up and helped me forward. I saw Dirks' handlers bringing him out to scratch. I went to meet them, my legs dragging horribly. I was in fear I hadn't the strength to strike another blow. But then I saw Dirks' face—or it had once been a face! Now it was battered beyond recognition.

He hung limp in the arms of his men. The Umpire spoke sharply to the men, and they let Dirks go. He stepped backward one pace, reeled in a half-circle, buckled suddenly and fell on his face in the broken turf . . .

I was stumbling away when the Umpire caught me. I leaned against him to keep from falling. He lifted my right arm, bellowing words that I could not understand, till suddenly they were drowned out with the shattering clamor that burst from the crowd.

MEN were leaping into the ring; they shoved me to and fro, wringing my hands, shouting things that had no meaning. Then Owain was beside me; he guided my lagging legs through the ropes. I was suddenly weak, and would have fallen but for ready hands that caught me.

The crowd swam before my eyes, but again from them all two figures stood out: the two had been with the prince when I first had seen him in the aisle—the white-haired old man and the boy beside him, with his face half hid by a topper low on his brow.

I said to Owain: "Let me away from here. I can hardly stand."

There were many willing hands to lift me and carry me through the noise of the mob, up the slope of the downs. I had not noticed till then that the sky was black with clouds and the wind blowing lustily. We were at our carriage, and the men put me down to my feet so that I could step into it.

And then again I saw at the edge of the crowd about me the two figures: the old man and the boy. I saw them stop before another brougham; the boy in the topper spoke briefly to the other, and then went into the brougham. The white-haired man was coming toward me.

He was within ten feet before I recognized him: *Phineas!*

And of a sudden new strength flowed into me. I knew what old Phineas was to tell me. I knew who the "boy" in the topper was! I threw off my supporters and staggered crazily to the brougham.

Just as I opened the door to climb in, there was a zigzag flash of lightning and a terrible clap of thunder. The rain was pelting down in torrents. But I was paying little attention to that. For two arms were about my neck and a mass of brown hair—disguised no more by the topper—was in my face.

Joyce was sobbing: "Dafydd—Dafydd! And I called you a coward! You will forgive me that, Dafydd?"

The door was yanked open, and old Owain stood staring. He pulled at my arm, pointing back to the crowd. "The Prince, Davey! His Highness—"

"Yes!" cried I; and I turned up Joyce's face. "There are explanations due, madam! You send me your token—by a prince!"

She was laughing. "Were you not proud, Dafydd? But 'twas simple. I was on my way to London this morning to see my uncle Adam—and in Mitcham I came upon the Prince's party, going to your fight. And—my uncle Adam was with them—so . . ."

But Owain was urging me. "The Prince has sent me, Davey. He wants to shake the hand of England's new champion!"

I peered out to where George Augustus stood, some fifty yards away, looking like some great sea lion in his dripping fur coat, a comical figure in the rain that pelted down on him.

But I pushed Owain back and made to close the door.

"You may convey to His Majesty my uttermost gratitude," I grinned. "But tell him, pray, that I have swooned—or that I have dropped dead! —Or," I shouted above the howl of the storm, "tell him the truth: that the hands of England's new champion are jolly well occupied, both of them, right now!"

And old Owain, peering into the brougham and seeing that this was so, grinned owlishly and slammed the door. Phineas whacked the horses' rumps with his reins, and with a great lurch we were off, bumping over the rutty road . . .

ΑΡΙΑΔΝΕ ΣΠΕΑΚΣ

(ARIADNE SPEAKS)

(FRAGMENTS OF CLAY TABLETS FOUND AT NAXOS)

by Clyde B. Clason

Illustrated by MAURICE ARCHBOLD, Jr.

DAUGHTER of kings am I, daughter of Minos, the sea-king. The sands of the shore are not more numerous than the galleys of my father, the great lord of the Double-Axe, and the nations of the earth pay tribute to us: east, Caria, Lycia, and the cities of the wolf-visaged Phoenicians; north to remote Thessaly and beyond Thessaly even to the tribes of the tattooed Thracians; west to the limit of the world. Yes, even the three-cornered island on the rim of the world, the island of the savage Sikels, pays us tribute. But on the south dwell the

Pharaohs and between them and the house of the Minos is peace and an old friendship, a friendship that has lasted a thousand years and more.

Looked I from the red-parchment window panes to see a stranger galley moored at the royal dock in the river before my father's palace. Smaller it was than our ships of Crete, having but seven oars to a side, and its sail was of black, an ominous color at which I wondered. Could it be some pirate? But no, for centuries the war-galleys of the Minos have kept clear our Green Sea of such rovers. The ship had come on business with my royal father, else would it have anchored in the harbor outside, and so thinking I went to my bath.

Stood I in the clay tub that rests in the room adjacent to my sleeping-chamber while Phaedra poured from a tall jar warm water over my naked body and anointed my skin with fragrant oils. And Phaedra arranged my hair in dark curls across the forehead and in ringlets from the temples, as is the palace fashion, and placed on my head a golden diadem. From the big carved chest by the wall she brought fresh clothing: a flounced skirt, sloping outward from my waist in a stiff cone to the floor, and a bodice with puffed sleeves that left bare my ivory shoulders. But not the breasts; that was the fashion of an older time, for they who came before us were less modest than we, though in their art so marvelous. And the bodice, the plaits of the skirt also, were trimmed with the precious dye grudgingly yielded by the seven-pointed shell-fish —purple, the color of kings.

Of purple also was the waistcloth of Talos, who entered the room to wait respectfully before me; the costly garment was broidered with four-petaled flowers of gold and bound tightly about his slim waist with a broad silver girdle. Naked above the waist, his lithe, bronzed body, but on his head the leather helmet with the plumed crest of the palace guard. And over his arm his great bronze shield, breast-high and curving about the body like the half of a round tower. Of such weight was the shield that both my arms scarcely sufficed to lift it, though Talos bore it with ease. Thus did my cousin appear as he addressed me on that morning so long ago.

"Daughter of kings, I sorrow to say that I am forced to remain on duty at Knossos today and may not ride with you in your chariot as we planned. For an Achaian ship has come unexpectedly to bring the tribute of Athens."

"Then must I go alone," I pouted, "since none there is worthy to take your place." But Talos looked not pleased.

"I beseech you, daughter of kings, to take another. Mettlesome and high-spirited are your chestnut stallions, for all that your slim hands hold their reins so firmly. And the thread of my life is bound with yours, as the woof with the warp in a loom."

I smiled to think that Talos should show such care for me, though he in all else so brave. "It shall be as you wish, my betrothed. But why flaunts the Athenian the black sail of a pirate galley?"

And Talos frowned. "A conceit of these Achaian barbarians, who dare thus to vent their displeasure at your royal father's modest tribute."

WENT I to the audience chamber of the Minos where sat my great father upon his glistening gypsum throne, wingless griffins rising from the painted river banks on the walls behind his head. The Minos held in his hand his tall gold sceptre: on his head his crown of peacock plumes, and looped across his bronzed and naked chest the heavy golden chain of fleur-de-lys, the design only the heaven-born may wear. And in the room was a stranger, who washed his hands at the stone tank opposite the throne as all must do before they may address the Minos.

A good head taller than our men of Crete was this stranger, and he was dressed not as they but wore a short skirt and a sleeved garment to cover his body above the waist while leaving bare his muscular forearms. His chin was not smooth-shaven, like those of our men, but adorned with a pointed yellow beard, and his long hair was yellow also, not black like the hair of Crete. His eyes were not dark like ours but sea-gray, and in his face was that which did not altogether displease me.

And the stranger flung a leathern bag, clinking with metal, before the throne of the Minos at the feet of my royal father.

"Behold the yearly tribute of Athens, O king, which I, Theseus, prince of the royal house, do myself deliver. And I came purposely to tell you that it is not fit that we of Athens should so demean ourselves. We are a proud people, and the tribute galls us."

I marveled that any dared speak so boldly to the king of lords and lord of kings. But my father took not offense.

"A proud people, prince of Athens, cannot afford to lose in warfare. But come, you could not look more downcast were this lifeless metal the bodies of seven strong Athenian youths and seven fair Athenian maids. We talk not of politics today, but my daughter shall drive you in her chariot throughout our city; yes, the daughter of kings herself shall drive you. And in the afternoon there shall be games and afterwards a feast. I, king of the sea and lord of the Double-Axe, have spoken."

MY CHESTNUT stallions were prancing impatiently before the palace as I came out its gate with the stranger. We stepped into the chariot's gold-plated body—just room for two to stand there—and I took the reins from the slave who held them. High-spirited were the proud horses, as Talos had said, but for their plumed manes and the sweep of their tails I loved them dearly. And they bore us like the wind down the broad paved highway.

Behind us the broad palace of Knossos, its white walls rising terrace above terrace, on each terrace level the greenery of palms and flowering shrubs showing against the gleaming stone in a manner beautiful to behold. Before us the town and its many houses of brick and of stone, all with windows of oiled parchment, tinted in many colors.

Our people thronged the foot-paths at either side of the highway. They pressed forward into the gutters of their streets; they crowded the flat roofs of their houses. Cheer rose upon cheer as my chariot thundered past, for beloved is the Minos of the sea and beloved his daughter, the divine Ariadne.

Behind us the town and before us the harbor. Here in the Green Sea anchored the square-sailed galleys of my father, mast behind mast, like the spears of an army of giants. And I thought proudly of the power and the wealth of the sea-monarch, my father.

"I am of ancient lineage also," said the Athenian to me. "Descendant I am of Cecrops, our first king, half snake and half man, who many centuries ago crawled across the Green Sea from Egypt."

And I wondered at the strange fancy which could thus twist a tale so simple, for the true manner in which Athens was founded is well known to us, preserved in the clay tablets of my father's royal library.

"First-born of Aegeus and Aithra is Theseus, heir to the royal house," he went on. "And Theseus has slain Sinis the pine-bender, Cercyon the wrestler, Sciron the foot-washer, and Procrustes the stretcher—giants all, but his might was greater than theirs. And he has slain the gray sow of Megara and the bull that laid waste the Marathon, which no other could slay."

But I held my hand across my mouth to conceal a yawn, for already I was weary of this barbarian's vain and child-like boasting.

IN THE afternoon were the games my royal father had promised, and our nobles flocked to the arena while was unloosed the great bull. A monster with horns the length of three hands it was, and much damage had it wrought to the olive groves of the Messara before our men took it with nooses and staves, as is our custom. And the bull pawed the ground and with its brazen voice bellowed like the roar of thunder. And Talos went alone in the arena to meet him.

Wore Talos only his purple waistcloth and buskins and no weapon carried he, either to assault or to defend himself. At a speed no horse could equal rushed the great bull upon the slight figure of my betrothed. And my heart leaped to my mouth, though five and twenty times have I witnessed Talos triumph.

Then Talos caught the cruel horn that would have gored him and let the jerk of the bull's great head lift him clear of the ground. Hung he there head downward over the muzzle, scorning to use hands to hold himself, one horn locked under his knee, the other beneath his armpit. Thus the monster carried my betrothed the length of the field, nor did all his great fury suffice to shake the unwanted rider. Then did the crowd cheer, for few there are who dare to do this thing, but more was yet to come. As the huge beast tossed high its kingly head, Talos gave a great leap and somersaulted through the air above the bull's long body, landing lightly on the ground unharmed, at which my heart mightily rejoiced.

So they led away the great bull of the Messara. And the stands broke into thunderous applause, for peerless was Talos and well beloved, and none clapped so loudly as my father the Minos.

"Is there one in Athens who could do so well?" he asked of the Achaian, who sat beside us in the royal box. Whereupon the brow of the Athenian grew dark.

"Our powerful bodies are not built for jumping-jack tricks, king of Crete. But put a sword in my hand and send me into the arena, and I will slay your great bull as surely as I killed the bull that laid waste the Marathon, a larger monster by far than this."

And the words of Theseus caused

"The stranger flung a leathern bag, clinking with metal, before the throne of Minos."

my father to frown. Ignorant you are of our customs, Achaian prince, or you would not speak so heedlessly. Know you that not with metal may the sacred animal be slaughtered."

"Then let your greatest champion meet me in the wrestling ring," said the Athenian, who smarted under my father's just rebuke. He looked downward contemptuously upon the slight figures of our men. "Your two greatest champions at the same time. Theseus will show you the art of wrestling of which now you cannot guess, for he has vanquished Sinis the pine-bender, Sciron the foot-washer, Cercyon the wrestler-king of Eleusis, and Periphetes of the iron club—giants all such as you cannot know of, you puny men of Crete."

My father frowned in a manner well-known to me.

"Let the Nubian be brought to meet this boaster."

"You speak in jest!" I cried. "The Nubian will kill the prince of Athens!" For six of our most skilled the giant black had thrown in the wrestling ring, and six more had he slain with blows of the *cestus,* so that in both sports he ruled now as undisputed king. A present to us from Egypt he was, taken prisoner in warfare and sent to the Minos by his well-wishing brother, the Pharaoh Amenhotep.

(Translator's note: Probably Amenhotep III, 1415-1380 B.C. This reference clearly fixes the period of Ariadne as Late Minoan II—roughly two centuries before the Trojan war.)

My father only smiled. "Is it not a pleasure," he whispered, "to see a braggart laid low by his own boasting? But worry not, my daughter, I will stop the combat before it has gone too far."

THEN Theseus laid by his sleeved upper garment, and I saw that his body was not bronzed by the sun like those of our men but white as ivory, though graceful and well-muscled. And my heart trembled in spite of the promise of my royal father, for not even the might of kings serves always to prevent a fatal outcome of a combat which may end in an eye's twinkling. And for all the boorishness of this barbarian prince, he seemed too fair to die.

Into the arena walked the Nubian, taller than Theseus, aye, and brawnier of chest. His white teeth flashed against his black skin as he grinned to acknowledge the plaudits of the crowd, for the negro was of good nature, though in the ring so terrible. But no smile did he have for Theseus, only a ferocious scowl. Hardly had they come together than he wrapped his huge arms about the waist of the Athenian and lifted him clear of the ground, holding him high in the air for all the crowd to see.

So the bodies of the two twined together, jet against ivory, and my heart came near to stopping its beating, for thus had I seen those powerful black arms press all of the breath from the bodies of three of our bravest. I called upon the Minos to stop the unequal combat, but as he was about to raise his royal hand in the signal, Theseus, lithe as an eel, twisted from the Nubian's grasp. Then followed what I would not believe had not my own eyes seen it, for Theseus flung the black wrestler, mighty as a very bull, over his shoulder, and the negro's massive body crashed to the floor with the noise that a bull's fall makes. Nor did he move thereafter, for the fall had broken his back.

So did we all applaud the skill of our Athenian visitor, and afterwards followed the banquet my father had promised. Of sea-food did we eat—mullet and oysters, parrot-fish and the white meat of the shelled crab. On the flesh of the wild boar did we feast, and on that of the heath-cock, the goat and the fatted ox. Cheeses were there from the milk of both the goat and the cow, and bread baked from millet flour, and honey, and fruits too numerous to mention: figs and dates and plums and quinces. And we drank our wine in golden cups upon the brims of which perched golden doves, wrought with the wondrous skill of the metal-worker's art.

AND so passed our days while the Prince of Athens visited at my father's royal house. But there came at last the day of my marriage with Talos, and glad I was to see it dawn. Phaedra arrayed me in a sea-green gown that hung in clouds like foam from my white shoulders. And on my feet she put shoes of glazed leather with heels and on my head a jeweled diadem—green was all, the color of our dear sea. Driven by thirty oars the royal galley clove the green waters to anchor, far beyond the harbor, at a spot where was the sea as clear as rock-crystal. And looking down into its blue-green depths, we saw strange sea-things: starfish and shell, the prickly tufts of urchins and the waving fronds of water plants. Then did my father, the royal Minos, monarch of all the lands but Egypt that fringe the Green Sea, begin our ancient ceremony. And first to Talos and to me he did say—

(Translator's note: There are several unfortunate lacunae in the text of these tablets. It is greatly to be deplored that Ariadne is not permitted to tell us more of the wedding ceremony then existing in the Cretan sea-empire, for we can only guess at the significance of the curious ring episode which follows.)

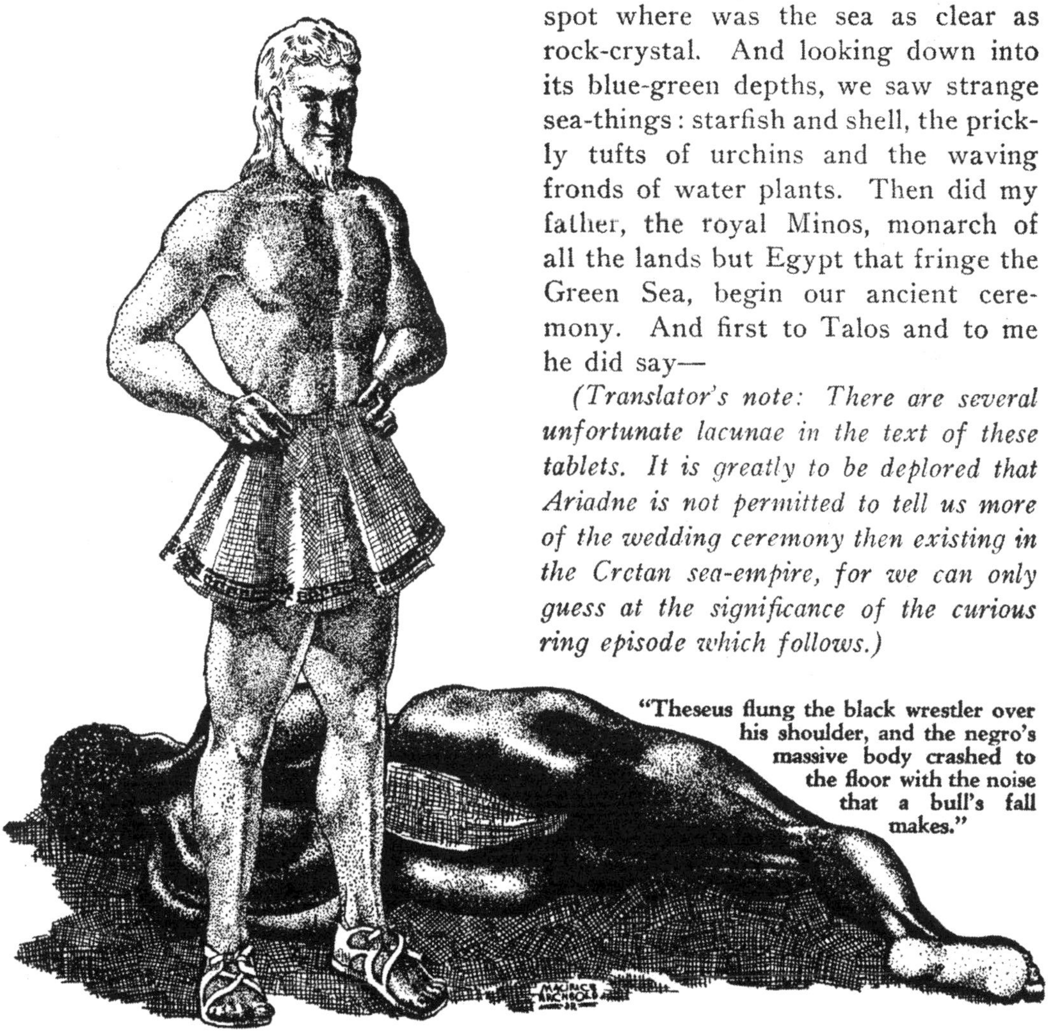

"Theseus flung the black wrestler over his shoulder, and the negro's massive body crashed to the floor with the noise that a bull's fall makes."

. . . then took the Minos his great signet from his finger, carved with the Double-Axe, that ancient, kingly symbol, which to us stands for the might of the God's thunderbolt. Green was its stone and of value incalculable, for it had been brought to the Minos from the mountains that lie east of the world.

(Translator's note: It appears almost inconceivable that Ariadne, a thousand years before the Age of Pericles, could refer to the jade workings in the Kuen-Lun mountains south of Khotan from which the jade of bronze-age China was mined. However, the commercial intercourse among prehistoric peoples was of wider extent than is generally realized. Schliemann, for instance, found jade axes at the site of Troy which could have come from no nearer source than Chinese Turkestan.)

Into the bosom of our great mother, the Sea, did the Minos throw his priceless ring, and it sank slowly, down, down, until it vanished from the sight of our eyes. And Talos, filling deep his lungs with air, sprang head-first over the side of the galley. Down he swam, straight as an arrow's flight, and so long he remained in the kingdom of the sea that we all marvelled. But finally my betrothed climbed back upon the deck of the great galley, and his face, I saw, was filled with shame and his finger barren of the ring of the Minos.

"It is caught in some crevice of a rock," I said to comfort him. "Rest, my beloved, and try again, and this time will the Goddess be kinder." But my heart was heavy within me, even as I spoke, for well I knew that the portent presaged some grave misfortune to us all. And, lo, while Talos was recovering his breath, Theseus the Athenian removed his sleeved upper garment and dived before any could prevent him into the green depths of the sea.

And surely was this Achaian the beloved of the Goddess, for when he returned to the deck, the priceless ring of the Minos showed upon his finger.

"Amphitrite is gracious!" he laughed, and tossed back the fair hair dripping to his shoulders. But we laughed not, for we were shamed: Talos and I and the kingly Minos.

And Talos would have slain the Achaian with the dagger he drew from his silver girdle, but I stayed my cousin's angry hand. And it were better that my lifeless body had been cast into the sea, for much evil was to come of this Athenian, as shall be related.

THEN, as we rowed back toward the harbor, did I see an unaccustomed sadness troubling the face of my father, the kingly Minos. "It is of no matter," I said to comfort him. "I may wed Talos another time, and then will the Goddess be kinder." But my father shook his kingly head.

"It is the action of the Achaian which troubles me, my daughter."

"Blame him not too much," I said, "for he is but a barbarian and ignorant of our customs. Else would he never have seized that destined for another man."

But my father, the great, the royal, the kingly Minos, shook his head and would not be comforted.

"A thousand years and more has our island-empire lasted," he said as he restored the green ring to his kingly finger. "Yet did it seem to me that I saw our proud sea-power slipping away at last, to fall into the hands of these fair-haired Achaians. For a thousand years, my daughter, make not one of eternity's days."

Then did the Athenian prince decide, tardily, that he had overstayed his welcome and make his preparations for departure. And on the following evening I came into the throne room to find him gaming with the Minos. Marvelous to behold was the gaming-board of my father; its frame, ivory; its pattern inlaid with ivory, too, and with gold and silver and crystal and blue *kyanos*. And upon its inlaid squares my father and Theseus dueled with silver counters.

But so unskilled was the Athenian that he could not keep his tongue from idle chatter while he played.

"The casks of water and the provisions are stored within my galley, O King of Crete, as are the gifts you make to my royal father."

And my father moved a counter to take two of those belonging to the Athenian. And I saw he intended a snare which the Athenian did not note.

"Even now my men are aboard the great galley, prepared to row away when the chariot of Phoebus first shows in the eastern sky."

"It is well," said my father briefly, for he liked not speech while he gamed. And he moved another counter.

"Shall I, King of Crete, bring word that the tribute so displeasing to our people will be lightened?" questioned Theseus. And so asking, he captured one of my father's pieces, nor heeded the snare which the cunning Minos had laid for him.

"The tribute must be paid in full, every jot and every tittle," answered the mighty lord of the Double-Axe. "And it shall be paid so long as my power is greater than yours of Athens." And my father swept from the board all of the remaining counters of the Achaian prince.

Sprang Theseus angrily to his feet. "Now, by the owl-shield of Pallas Athene, I game no more! And the tribute shall be paid until we learn how to strive against the power of the Pelasgians and their bull-god the Minotaur."

THEN did the Minos leave us to go to another part of the palace, and I sat upon the throne of the Pointed Arch, which only my father or I might occupy. By my side the son of Aegeus and Aithra sat upon a stone bench, and soft were the words he spoke to me.

"Daughter of kings, though you are dark yet are you fair—the fairest maid by far in all the lands kissed by the Green Sea."

He laughed hugely at his cumbersome riddle, but I frowned. Ill did it become this Achaian lordling to speak thus familiarly to the daughter of kings. Yet was he tall, and in all things did bear himself as a prince.

"Happy would be my heart could I but bear you as my bride to the halls of my father's house."

Then was I angered beyond words at his barbarian insolence.

"Wed you, Achaian? Not while one Cretan remains in our island-empire whom I might take in preference. For the very least of our nobles is your superior."

The Athenian, a simple man who spoke always his mind, could not know that it was his plain, blunt speech which caused my displeasure. Nor would I tell him, for my heart was still angry within me. Then he tossed back his head, flinging over his shoulders his great mane of yellow hair.

"Have care, princess, lest I muster all the strength of Athens to end this hateful tribute. Lest an Athenian fleet sack the palace of kings, while I take for my own the betrothed of Talos."

Then did the throne room ring with my scornful laughter.

"A fleet from Athens! It would be beaten back with slaughter before it reached the first of our island outposts. So would the tribute you dislike be doubled, aye and trebled, while you yourself were condemned to die. And this you know as well as I, son of Aegeus and Aithra."

"It is true," he owned, and upon his face sadness where before anger had been. "We cannot strive with the bull-headed god of the Pelasgians. Thus is the daughter of kings as far from my reach as the jewel-glittering Pleiades, for all that I love her so deeply. The people of Athens fear the Minotaur, and even Theseus fears him, though he dreads nothing mortal."

A tenderness arose within me as I saw him, who had been so proud, now so humble. "Why do you of Athens so fear the Minotaur?" I asked.

"Because it is a monster," he replied. "Body of a man it has, though taller than any man now living, and above its body the head of a mighty bull. With its great horns it gores the flesh of youths and with its thick lips it drinks the blood of tender maidens. And they say the monster is kept in a winding maze, cunningly contrived so that he cannot escape, else would he dethrone the Minos and rule the land of Crete."

I smiled at your naive simplicity, O Theseus!

"Tonight, Prince of Athens, you shall see him with your own eyes."

Evil was my heart to counsel me thus, and evil came of it, as I shall relate.

SO VAST a ground covered the palace of Knossos, so many its halls, its courts, its broad staircases, its winding corridors, that even I might lose myself in it, yes even the daughter of kings. But one man knew its turnings well, and him I took with us: Daidalos, the palace architect; his the mad genius which had wrought for us the wondrous dancing-ground without the walls.

Naught was there man could do which Daidalos could not better, yet in his madness he sought to excel the birds as well and would make for himself great wings of wax which he hoped would bear him swiftly through the air. And all of his attempts at flight had met with the failure to be expected, yet so sensibly did he speak of his great folly that few would guess the Goddess had uprooted the seat of his reason.

"Of no other material than wax can they be moulded and therein lie grave difficulties. For if I fly too low the spray of the sea will spoil my brave inventions, and if too high the rays of the jealous sun will melt them and cause the wax to drip away. Thus am I troubled, but a larger matter is it that the wax of the bee is costly, and I, O daughter of kings, am a poor man and lack the funds to purchase it in the large quantities needed."

So spoke Daidalos, but I kept my face averted and heeded not his many hints. Well known to us all was the cupidity of the architect and the subject of many a palace jest. Yet his faults were easily forgiven when we trod upon our noble dancing-ground, for nothing like it has—but, lo, how the foolish mind does wander! It is not of dancing that I wish to write.

And the walls of the corridors through which we passed on that night are decorated with pictures: scenes in many colors of the chase and the harvest; of the *cestus* and the bull-leaping; of our dances and the long processions gravely winding their way to the sacred shrine of the Goddess. Painted all are they with the very breath of life, by an ancient skill that is now lost to us, and valued mightily by our art-loving people, yet Theseus heeded them not.

And the Athenian could have seen all clearly, had it been in his mind to look upon our glorious frescoes, for in every corridor tall lamps of stone stood at frequent intervals. Atop its fluted column each stone basin held three or four wicks to drink greedily of the oil therein, while the smoky flames rendered brilliant the palace of my father. And other works did Theseus pass without noting: bronze amphorae from which the lamp-flame glinted at every turning. Taller than a man was each, and of graceful shape, and on them the smiths had graved a skillful pageantry, so that the whole of our people's history might be read upon the metal long after our noble writing has been forgotten. But Theseus heeded them not, and I marveled to see a man so blind to beauty.

Yet did he bear himself as a king's son should.

NOW we came to the *labyrinth,* the name meaning in our language "Place of the Double-Axe," the great *labrys* itself being painted upon its cypress door. "Here, Athenian," I laughed, "is the winding maze in which the bull-god of the Cretans is confined, lest he escape and dethrone the Minos. So summon all your courage, for we go to visit him."

Daidalos took from his belt a bronze key, which stirred the Athenian to greater wonder than all the frescoes of the corridors. Never had he seen a lock before and did not understand how the key could open it, though to us the contrivance is but simple. And after he had opened the door, Daidalos brought a torch to light the wicks of the stone lamps so that the Place of the Double-Axe might shine before us in all its splendor.

Few temples do we have in Crete, for we are not as priest-ridden Egypt, yet some there are, and this one: a great hall, longer by far than it is broad and divided lengthwise by twin rows of cypress columns. Massive forest giants these tall columns were before the axes of our woodsmen laid them low and our carpenters shaped them into pillars of perfect roundness and fluted them with the spiral curve that to us symbolizes eternity, since it does ever recede from its beginning. Each column rests upon a broad base of green serpentine, and each is topped by a huge round capital, so that the sight of these twin rows of great pillars is one marvelous to behold. And midway between them, at the far end of the hall, sat in his throne the great son of our Blessed Mother.

Figure greater than man was he, such as few of our sculptors have ever learned to carve, though in Egypt the art is understood well. Body of man did he have, wrested by the sculptor's chisel from a huge block of black steatite, but his head was that of a bull. And to us the bull symbolizes the wrath of Storms and Earthquakes so dreaded by our fathers in olden times.

And this carving was of that ancient art of which I spoke, the head, especially, breathing the very breath of life. The black nostrils were inlaid with the creamy white of shells, and the eye-sockets set with rock crystals, colored with red and yellow, in a secret way now lost to us, to imitate the light and dark circlets by which we see. And the great stone head was hollow, a hole being bored at the back of the neck and continuing through the mouth, so that there could protrude through the lips the shaft of our sacred weapon, the great *labrys.*

"BEHOLD the Minotaur!" I laughed, pointing to the stone statue. "This is the bull-god of Crete whom you Athenians so dread. Do you not fear him now, O Achaian prince?"

"Nay," Theseus answered somberly, "I fear him not." So speaking, he drew from the neck of the image, the great Double-Axe, our sacred *labrys.* While I watched in horror, he swung the mighty weapon, and its bronze blade clanged against the stone of our wondrous image.

And strength more than human was in his arm, for at one blow the marvelously carved head toppled to the stone flagging. Broken was the black head of the god, and shattered his eyes of crystal! And the Prince of Athens laughed exultantly at the sight.

"Divine Ariadne, now is the tribute of my city ended. For Theseus has slain the Minotaur, the bull-god from which came the power of insolent Crete."

"You have slain no god!" I cried. "The gods, Theseus, dwell far apart and are forever beyond your reach. Nevertheless, you have sinned more grievously than you can know. For you have destroyed a work of our ancient art, and for that offense the penalty is death throughout my father's dominions."

But as I pronounced his doom, confusion overcame my senses. Confusion I had never known, even at the words of my dear Talos. "You will die," I faltered, but Theseus only laughed and made the great axe whistle in the air.

"What care I for death with this good weapon in my hand? If one comes, I will slay, and if two come, I will slay, and if twenty come, I will slay them all."

"O man of blood!" I cried. "How like a foolish child you speak and act! You cannot slay twenty, but if you could, then would twenty more come, and twenty after them, so very soon would your slaughter be ended. So put away our sacred *labrys,* and you, Daidalos, run not to inform the palace guard, as I see is your intent, until I take counsel with the Mother of All."

WENT I to the pillared shrine of She whose signs are the Snake and the Dove. Her serpents were gold, twined about her ivory forearms, and I raised my eyes from them to look upon her grave, sweet face. So She, who rules the earth and the air, the sea and the mountains, told me the course I should follow.

Final are the decrees of the Goddess and cannot be gainsaid, but I did weep a little as I turned from her pillared shrine. Dear to me was Talos, dear to me my father the Minos, and unwanted the love for this stranger the Goddess had put in my heart. Yet would I not betray it.

So I went to the Athenian. "Theseus, son of Aegeus and Aithra, is it in your heart to deal fairly with me, to make me your true and honorable wife?"

And he sank upon one knee and lifted my hand reverently to his lips.

"While I watched in horror, he swung the mighty weapon."

"Daughter of kings, it is in my heart to deal fairly with you, to make you my true and honorable wife. Yes, by the owl-shield of Pallas Athene!"

From my fingers I took rings and from my forearms bracelets of gold and from my upper arms broad bands of silver—inset all with gems whose price was beyond compare. And these I laid in the hands of Daidalos.

"Skilled architect, is there a way by which we may depart from the palace and reach the Athenian ship without passing my father's guards?"

But Daidalos hesitated, at which Theseus growled and brandished his huge axe.

"Speak, fellow, or die."

But I stayed the strong hand of my Achaian lover. And from my neck I took a golden chain and from my hair my glittering diadem. These, too, I laid in the outstretched hands of greedy Daidalos, and then he did answer me.

"There is such a way, O daughter of kings, and I am one of the few who know it. Come, I will show you."

And Daidalos led us to a great stone that moved, and when he lifted it there was exposed a ladder staircase.

"This, daughter of kings, is one of the hidden entrances to the drains which lie below your father's palace. And from this shaft, by stooping low, you may walk on hands and knees through the cement-lined conduit to the river where the Athenian ship is moored."

But I knew that once the moving stone had fallen above our heads we would be plunged in a darkness more profound than even the awesome gloom of the Dictaean cave, which only the heaven-born Minos may penetrate. And I suspected a snare of greedy

Daidalos, thinking he might deem my father would reward him with more than the gold and jewels he had received of me. So I stayed my feet from following Theseus, who had rushed straightway down the ladder staircase.

"Is it not true, palace architect, that the drains cross in many directions?"

He bowed his head in answer. "Daughter of kings, it is true."

"Then how may we succeed in reaching the river? In the vast underground maze beneath the palace floors we might creep for days, nor find the exit."

"O divine Ariadne!" laughed Daidalos. "Your doubts are well founded, yet is the answer simple. In the conduit is even now a runnel of water which flows ever downward until the river is reached. And the direction of its flow shall lead you, as surely as a clue of thread, to the Athenian ship."

"If you betray us," Theseus growled from below, "your head, Daidalos, shall be the first to feel the weight of the great axe with which I slew the Minotaur. And though you were protected by a hundred fighting men, yet would my vengeance claim you."

But Daidalos answered, "Peace, O Prince of Athens! It is not in my heart to betray you or the divine Ariadne, for whose wit and whose courage I have boundless esteem." And I knew he spoke truth.

SO WE permitted Daidalos to lower the moving stone above our heads and descended the ladder staircase to crawl on hands and knees through the cement-lined conduit. More terrible was the darkness than any I had dared imagine, but Daidalos had prophesied truly, for the runnel of water led us as surely as a clue of thread to the river. Thus were we able to escape the guards of my father and board the Athenian ship.

Then Theseus woke his sleeping men and bade them weigh the bronze anchor and pull with all the strength of their arms down the river before the ships of the Minos could be aroused in swift pursuit. And the barbarians obeyed gladly the commands of their prince, for their hearts were sick with longing for the mud huts of their native Athens.

Yet were we not to escape unhindered, for as we passed the tall tower which commands the approach to the palace, my cousin Talos leaped downward upon the galley's deck. On his left arm he carried his curved bronze shield, in his right hand a long sword, and in his eyes was the terrible lust of battle.

"Is it thus, Prince of Athens, that you would repay the hospitality of my great lord? Dare you by force to carry away his divine daughter? For this shameful deed, barbarian, you shall surely die."

Brave was Talos, and my heart ached for him, alone among so many foemen. For he alone had noted the departure of the black-sailed galley, and the men of Athens plied their oars lustily and were driving the galley far from the guard tower so that a call for aid could not be heard by those within. And the brawny Theseus towered a head above the slender figure of my cousin. And, although Talos carried a sword and shield and was well skilled in their use, the Athenian bore the great bronze *labrys,* the terrible weapon before which every man, unless dearly beloved by the Goddess, must surely fall. So I stepped at once between them.

"Sheathe your sword, my cousin, for of my own will I go to become the bride of Theseus."

Cruel were my words, though in my heart was but the intent to save my cousin's life, and Talos hung his head.

"Speak you the truth? Then am I shamed before all men. Yet while breath remains within my body, I shall not suffer an Achaian to pluck from the crown of the Minos its most-prized jewel."

Then was my heart sad indeed, for nothing could now avert the combat between these so dear to me. So I stood apart while they fought on the swaying deck. And the men of Athens pulled with all their strength for the open sea, knowing well their very lives were the stake of this race.

THRICE did Theseus swing his heavy axe, thrice and more, and always did Talos lithely evade him. Peerless he was in the arts of war as peerless in the bull-ring! And the sword of Talos flicked like a brazen serpent into the side of the Athenian, and his blood gushed in a crimson stream, a grievous sight at which I cried aloud.

"Fear not, O daughter of kings," called Theseus, and swung once more his axe. But again Talos stepped lightly aside, so that the blade, although it missed his leathern helmet by hardly more than the breadth of a single hair, crashed harmlessly to the deck. And so much might had Theseus put into the blow that the great blade bit deep into the timbers of the deck, and even the powerful arm of the Athenian could not dislodge it.

Then Talos could have delivered the death stroke, yet hesitated, for it is not the training of our soldiers to slay an unarmed foe. "Barbarian, you are at my mercy!" he cried. "Yield now, or you die."

"I yield not," returned Theseus, and, bracing his sinewy legs against the deck, with all the strength of his body, he pulled free the bronze *labrys*. Tardily, then, did Talos smite, and the Athenian's blood spurted forth from a fresh wound as he swung the axe again.

Weakening was Theseus from his many wounds, and Talos as yet untouched. But the foot of my cousin slipped upon the very blood himself had caused, and he failed at last to elude the axe's swing. His curved shield he held before him to take the blow, but the terrible weapon of Theseus clove the metal like a thing of parchment, and Talos fell backwards into the deepening waters of the open sea. Nor did he rise again.

My heart wept for Talos, my dear cousin, who but for the whim of the Goddess had been my husband, but the heart of Theseus exulted.

"I have slain the giant Talos," crowed he, while I bandaged the deep wounds which the sword of my slender cousin had wrought. "Man of bronze was Talos, and the touch of his red-hot body slew all who approached him. Yet yielded he to the might of Theseus, and the hissing of ten thousand serpents arose from the sea as its waters quenched the flames of the bronze giant's body."

NOW was the galley's black sail unfurled, and a breeze drove us speedily from the island of Crete and its hundred cities. And as we ploughed the green waters, Theseus made words for his oarsmen to sing, to a tune common at my father's court.

"Theseus has slain the Minotaur, the bull-god of the Pelasgians. Seven youths and seven maidens we were forced to send as tribute for the monster, and Theseus among their number. But the divine Ariadne, enamoured of his prowess, led him to the room of the Minotaur and placed in his hands the weapon by which he might slay. Then, with a clue of thread, she guided him safely through the mazes of the labyrinth, and he slew also the bronze man Talos as he sought to crush the ship between his giant fingers. Beloved of the gods is Theseus, the very blood of Pallas Athene, and beloved is he also by the daughter of kings."

So sang Theseus, and wonder it was that I could so care for one to whom the spirit of truth was stranger. Yet in his love-making was he not untender.

Swiftly as a swallow's flight, the breeze blew our galley to the Isle of Naxos. Here might we tarry to procure food and water, for the ships of the Minos come to this isle but seldom, and at Naxos Theseus became, in truth, my husband. And our hearts were glad within us as we lay together; so strange it was to see in the morning, when my kiss awoke him, that his face was doleful.

And I pressed my lips against his and asked, "Why is the heart of my dear lord so sorrowful? Is not Ariadne now his bride?"

"O daughter of Minos," he answered me, "I may not bring you with me to Athens, lest I cause the death of my royal father, King Aegeus. This I saw in a dream last night, and dreams speak truly, as all men know, for they are portents sent to us by Zeus the Thunderer."

Powerless were my words to prevail against his barbarian superstitions, yet in his way he tried to comfort me.

"The dream did not say, divine Ariadne, that afterwards I might not send for you. So wait you here, and as soon as I reach Athens I will dispatch a ship. Yes, I swear it, by the owl-shield of Pallas Athene!"

Thus was I forced to be content, and the black galley of Theseus left me alone among the folk of Naxos. Great reverence do these good people show to the daughter of kings, yet is their simple life wearisome to one who has known the splendor of my father's court. So to beguile the time I asked for clay, and this they brought at my command. And in a stone bowl I moistened with water the clay lumps, and with my own hands kneaded the tablets.

And the ships of the Minos come not to find me.

With a reed, plucked from the river's edge and sharpened to a point, do I inscribe in the moist clay the record of these things. But as I write the thought comes that, if these tablets lie too long buried, men may never know my history.

For should our proud sea-empire fall, as my father fears it may, then is the art of writing lost with us. Ignorant of our cultured Minoan script are the barbarian Achaians. Rude and illiterate are the black-bearded Phoenicians.

Only in Egypt is something of the art known.

Thus wait I, O Theseus, for the ship you promised so faithfully to send. And it comes not, though three times has the rising moon changed its shape from disk to crescent.

Can it be that Ariadne is forgotten?

Mojave Gunpowder

There were four of them, great hairy men, riding slumped down on their horses.

by Gilbert Eldredge

***Illustrated by* JAY JACKSON**

HIGH on its peg in the thick 'dobe wall hung the big powder horn, longer than a man's arm, its great mouth toward the Rancho de Santa Monica and the sea, its sharp glossy point toward the brazier of glowing charcoal against the south wall and the sleepy Pueblo de Los Angeles. A little lower hung the small horn for hunting. Little Conchita could just touch it with the tips of her tiny fingers but Eduardo, fourteen, could swing it over his shoulder like a grown caballero. "Just to scare off robbers," John Dermot would say teasingly to his plump young wife, his hand affectionately patting the great horn. "They'll never know 'tis not filled with good New York powder instead of this fizzy stuff from the Mojave that won't carry a ball through a green chili pepper."

"In California we have no robbers," she would say. "Only thin gringos who steal my puchas when baked fluffy and well sprinkled with sugar, Don Juan Flaco, Mr. Skinny John."

"Donwhanflaco," giggled little Conchita.

"Senora the fat lady!" He kissed his wife as though she were still the lithesome Maria of the snapping castanets and the twinkling feet. She blushed slightly, her feet tapping the opening steps of a fandango then gliding into the more sensuous jarabe.

They looked young to have a fourteen year old son; too handsome and light-hearted. He, tall, very dark in the hair, very gray in the eye, with gay regular features, almost feminine except for the fixed set to the mouth and a little gravish look of responsibility. You recognized that breed of gentlemen—the Wild Geese of Ireland. She showed her Hispano-California ancestry—full-faced, red-lipped, her long blue-black hair held high with a gleaming tortoise-shell comb. Her face, brown like the husk of her cigarette, glowed warm and coquettish now; later it would set in the stern bustling lines of authority when managing the household and calling thin sharp orders to los Indios servants.

Now Eduardo, a little replica of his father, followed to the tras corral, and watched intently as Don Juan Dermot gave orders to the vaqueros for el rodeo and the butchering of the beef. The meat must be cut in strips just so, to cure for the carne seca or jerky.

Eduardo asked, "Aren't you going to make powder today, father?"

John looked down into the thin serious dark face. "I'll be making a chemist of you yet," he chuckled. "Come! Perhaps this day the powder will bang, not fizzle." In the tiny 'dobe hut between the tortillera and the barbecue pit they pored over their formulas. Saltpetre from the Mojave, Sicilian sulphur, and dogwood charcoal lay on the slab table.

OUTSIDE a slow drizzling rain sank deep into the dried clay bricks. Wet sand spurted as six men rode up the path and into the corral, the water glistening from each lacquered black hat above the bright-colored serapes and gleaming from the metal points of their twelve-foot lances.

"Senor, los lanceros are here!" a vaquero called.

John appeared quickly in the doorway. "Buenos Dias le de Dios!" he greeted jovially.

"Buenos Dias, old friend!" they called joyfully. "We have much news."

They dismounted, handing their reins to an Indian servant, leaning the long lances with the gay handkerchief pennants against the corral wall. Cocks were produced. Shouting, laughter, the calling of bets and encouragement to the cocks echoed up from the corral as Andres Montalvo followed John to the house. Dona Maria produced fiery brandy in Boston glassware while the two men squatted on their heels on the big bearhide. They toasted each other in silence.

"You know of the affairs in the north?" Andres began doubtfully. "The gringo Fremont has proclaimed his Bear Republic, then repudiated it. The United States and Mexico are at war. Los Angeles is garrisoned with Americanos."

"Si! I know." John's lips tightened.

"Last night we friends of California held a junta in an old wine cellar at Paradon Blanca. We organized a company of lancers and in a night attack drove out the Americanos under Captain Gillespie. A few tossed on lance points. No serious loss of life on either side."

"I had not heard."

"You are extranjero, a foreigner." Andres looked his friend full in the eyes. "Are you one of us?"

John bore the intense gaze unflinchingly, his gray eyes steady. "I left Ballyvaghan, Ireland, a poor immigrant boy of twelve. I sweated six years in Yankee Boston preparing our California hides for the shoemakers. Our hides and tallow have helped make Boston great, mi amigo. I starved on mouldy pork in the China-packet trade and smuggled opium from Mangalore to Monaco."

"A strange life, my friend."

"When I rounded the Horn with a Halifax bluenose I thought I would die in the storms. California seemed like heaven itself. I deserted the ship at San Pedro and here I am." He laughed aloud at the wonder of it all.

"We may all be killed. The Yankees shoot straight."

"It is a chance. I am a Californian, a father, a land-owner. I will be a lancero with you, my friend. I can handle a lance."

"With the best." They drank to California in aguardiente.

"MUST we fight all with the lance? Have we no good powder?" John had no illusions as to the might and tenacity of the young Republic of the United States.

"Three rounds for the cannon. A few pinches for the pistolas. Who cares?" Andres shrugged light-heartedly. "The lance is a gentleman's weapon."

"If I had only started my experiments sooner. My powder fizzles also." John tried to shove to the rear of his mind the picture of eighty laughing carefree lancers, without artillery, muskets or powder, pitted against the trained and almost inexhaustible army of the United States. "I guess the Mojave saltpetre is bad," he continued lamely.

Andres lifted his glass of aguardiente laughing. "Viva California! Viva la guerra! Adelante amigo! Hurry! Dress and join us." He bowed gravely to Dona Maria, clicked his heels along the hard-beaten floor of the casa until his spurs jingled musically, and rejoined his camaradas in the corral.

Dona Maria looked up a little fearfully at her tall husband. "Where are you going, Juan?"

"To fight with the lanceros. It is only a gesture I think."

"I am afraid. This Captain Merrit and his band of gringo cut-throats, where are they?

"Far to the north I understand." He was hastily pulling a fine white hand-worked camisa over his head, and adjusting the tight black trousers, calzoneras de paño, slit midway up the leg. A gold-braided black vest and a black silk camora on his head completed the costume. He wondered whether the lancers would stand against gun-fire, and how many would return.

Maria had stuffed carne seca and tortillas into a saddle-bag with pan dulce, sweet bread, on top. He looked so handsome and brave in his traje charro. Her eyes swam with fear for him.

He glanced down at her, a little frown between his eyes. "You mustn't worry, querida mia. Merrit and his cut-throats are far away. And anyway, we'll be around somewhere."

"I will not worry. I have Eduardo and the Indian servants."

"Brave girl!" He bent and kissed her lingeringly. Her arms were tight around his neck. Conchita giggled. Eduardo stood proudly in the doorway holding the long lance.

"Mi padre," he laid a timid hand against his father's arm. "Perhaps while you are gone I can make the powder?"

John glanced quizzically down at the thin earnest face and his smile softened. "Of course," he said hastily. "I had forgotten. Of course you will make it."

A voice from the corral carried through the thick adobe walls. "Adelante compañero! Hurry!"

"Coming! Pronto!" John shouted and seized the lance. "I will be back tomorrow perhaps, or next day." He ducked his head through the hole in his serape and adjusted the tight thick wool about his shoulders. Through the open door a sea breeze whirled the rain until it hissed against the hot charcoal brazier. The lanceros were lining up in squadron formation, the water running in tiny streams from hat brims and dripping soggily from the serapes onto the steaming horses. Dona Maria saw the flash of white teeth and the shine of the water on the gleaming lance heads. "Viva California! Viva la guerra!" they shouted.

CHAPTER II

JOHN had mounted and swung his Arabian cream gelding into line. They splashed off down the road until the live oaks and laurels hid them at the bend. Maria stood staring after them while the rain-drops sparkled on her long lashes and her bodice felt wet and cold. Then she closed the door and the little house seemed suddenly damp and smoky and lonesome.

Conchita was pretending to read the carved name-plate by the door. "Why do we call this El Rancho Pinacate?"

"A silly notion of your father's," Maria answered absently. "Pinacate is the little doodle-bug that stands on its hands on the seashore at Santa Monica."

"Eduardo, play marbles with me," Conchita demanded.

"Marbles!" said Eduardo scornfully. "You should be helping mama make pinole." He glanced shyly at his mother. He wanted to tell her that he would save her from the gringo robbers, but something in her face kept him silent.

She said suddenly. "Eduardo, dig little sister a tiny pozito in the corner and find her some chilicotes for marbles."

Eduardo dug a very small hole in one corner of the hard packed floor and opened a green chilicote pod for the big round seeds. Then he went outside to the bodega and brought back the long strips of dried salted jerky. He pounded them soft and laid them beside the tortillas on the metal top of the open grate comal. The rain hissed and steamed from the hot metal and he poked more wood underneath. No cooking was done inside. There was a constant coming and going from the house to the comal under its partial roof-covering just outside the door. His mother ground the big red chilis on the metate, sliced onions, green chilis, tomatoes, and garlic; then dropping the slightly roasted jerky into an iron pot followed it with drippings and the prepared vegetables. This and tortillas would be the evening meal.

"May I make powder now, mother?"

"I wanna play powder with brother."

"Eduardo may work in the powder house. Conchita will help me with nistamal," she said evenly. "No nonsense now, muchachita! You may knead the dough and make the little balls. I will show you how to clap them between your hands until they are thin like pancakes."

Conchita had found a snail clinging tight to a tomato vine. "Daddy calls them sheleg-a-bookie. Why mama?"

"It is not Spanish; Irish perhaps," Maria said doubtfully. "I think it means something about a snail with a hump."

CHAPTER III

EDUARDO slipped his serape over his shoulders. He must be a man now and through with women's non-

Two Indian vaqueros squatted in the lee of the wall rolling innumerable cigarillos.

sense. "Call me, mama, if—if anything happens."

"Of course, Eduardo."

He looked once more at her face and closed the door softly. Outside the wind whipped around the tras corral and threw the rain in thin stinging sheets against his face. The barbecue pit was a small well of water. Two Indian vaqueros squatted in the lee of the wall rolling innumerable brown husk cigarillos. Good men on a horse to help at the rodeo and for cutting up the meat, but cowed and useless in a fight, he thought. Indian women were dropping unslaked lime into a caldero, adding maize and boiling it until the hulls rubbed off easily. This made a kind of hominy that could be ground smooth on the metate to a wet sticky dough for tamales or tortillas.

Inside the powder-hut he shook the water from his eyes and hung the serape on a wooden peg. From the box he took a handful of dry wood and struck flint and steel in the little round fireplace. A real wood fire in the house, with an outside chimney that drew, was a Yankee innovation but he liked to hear the crackle of the flames and besides it was useful for roasting the charcoal. He hummed a carol in a boyish falsetto voice:

"Somos Los Pastores que venomos adorar El Nino!

El Nino que ha nacido!"

He opened a gourd full of the dirty brownish-black gunpowder from an old experiment. The saltpetre was still in partial crystals and silky tufts just as they had found it in an alkali sink in the desert. He stirred it thoroughly with his finger and poured a charge down the throat of the little brass cannon that had come up from Mexico with Father Junipero. He rammed home a heavy wad of ejote fibers, primed the fire-hole, and pointed the muzzle towards the hills through a hole in the north adobe wall. He ran a hand lovingly along the scarred and dented brass and fingered the lions on the Spanish coat-of-arms. The cannon was short and plump and very small, intended more to astonish the Indians with the clap of thunder and dirty black smoke than for field operations.

HE CHARRED a stick in the fire and applied the glowing end to the touch-hole. The priming caught, the brass breech stirred, then writhed with a curious twisting motion along the floor. A long drawn s-s-s-shing sound like the escape of steam poured out with the black smoke from the muzzle. Two tears rolled down his cheeks, partly from disappointment, partly from the biting sting of the slow-burning powder. He opened the door to clear the smoke and let the rain cool his burning face. "Wouldn't even blow the wadding across the corral," he muttered, and kicked with his toe against the soft adobe wall.

The room cleared gradually of smoke and he closed the door. His father had always stuck tight to the old Roger Bacon formula—saltpetre 41.2, charcoal 22.2, sulphur 11.1 and this was the usual result. Eduardo kicked hard again and then nursed his buckskin-shod toe. In the corner he looked over his own experiments—saltpetre and alkali, dissolved in wood-ash lye and filtered. He gathered a measure of the crystals and deposited them on the table. From the fireplace he drew the precious metal cylinder where he had been roasting aged willow-wood. His father liked dogwood charcoal but Eduardo stubbornly stuck to willow. It has more body, he thought.

He powdered the charcoal and weighed it with the saltpetre. It came out seventy-five per cent saltpetre, fifteen per cent charcoal. He added ten parts of sulphur and grimaced at the result. The formula was wild, audacious, bizarre; but why not? This Roger Bacon was probably an Irishman who lived a long time ago. It was time a true Californian, a gente del pais, thought for himself.

The elation of discovery and invention went to his head like wine. Proudly he surveyed the heap of dirty brown powder and mixed it with ceremonious thoroughness. This made his hands black and brought on a second idea. He brought rain-water from the big hogshead at the corner of the house and sprinkled it over the new gunpowder. Then his heart sank. It's ruined now, he thought. All wet and ruined. He touched it gingerly. It felt sticky like dough, only not so smooth. Almost mechanically he shaped it into round balls and patted them between his hands until they spread out thin like tortillas. They looked very like Conchita's mud pies and he was of a mind to throw them away. Papa would laugh. Finally he spread them out on the slab table and washed his hands.

BACK in the house he found sister still tossing marbles at the hole he had dug in the corner. Mama was making atole de trigo gruel from wheat meal. He borrowed the long kitchen knife that had come all around the Horn from Boston, and returned to the powder room. The mud pie tortilla-looking pancakes were lying just as he had left them, a little black rim of moisture beginning to spread out and soak into the hard live-oak slabs. He took the knife and began chopping them very fine, cross-hatching until they looked like a coarse horse-comb.

Eduardo could hear his mother calling shrill orders to the Indian servants and issuing food to the women. From this and the growing murkiness he knew that it was time for their own dinner. He gave a last look at the chopped cakes on the table, wrapped his serape about his shoulders and returned to the house. He sat down to the table in his father's place and the Indian maid brought in the tortillas hot from the open grate comal just outside the door. He took the thin warm tortilla, folded it around his hand to form a funnel, pinched the end and passed it to his mother to fill with chopped meat and vegetables for sister.

Darkness closed in on them suddenly like the dropping of a curtain. From his chair Eduardo could see the corral wall, slate-gray through the drizzle, slowly fade to a velvety brown shadow. The laurel bushes just showing over the top seemed like black ghosts wagging their heads loosely from side to side. He closed the door softly. He could see that his mother was nervous.

"Time for bed," Dona Maria said suddenly.

Conchita began her usual wail. "I don't want to go to bed. Just one story and then I'll go."

"You must say your prayers first, or I will not tell you a single story."

"It's so cold, mama."

"It will be warm in bed."

"Can Eduardo sleep with me?"

"We all sleep in the same room. Hurry now! Get on your nightgown."

CHAPTER IV

THE two children slept in the north room under the slope of the great thatch roof; their parents across from them on the patio side. On cold nights they could see the glow of the charcoal fire reflected dully on the plastered mud ceiling, the long strings of chili peppers and maize, swaying in the drafts like gringo cut-throats advancing and retreating. Muffled through the thick walls they could hear the wail of a lone coyote on the Santa Monica hills or hear the swish of el coche jabalino, the wild boar, grubbing along the patio walls.

The room was cold and damp from the wet sun-dried bricks and the dampness that rose from the hard-beaten clay floor. The wind howled with soft musical overtones around the rush-thatched roof; the sound coming muffled and mysterious through the thickness of the thatch and more shrilly through the drafty crevices between the roof and walls.

Conchita crouched behind the hot brazier on the bearskin, wriggling her small plump body out of her one-piece dress and into her long woolen nightie, plumping down to her knees with a soft little thud and gabbling her prayers. She leaped expertly from the bearskin to the bullhide beside her bed.

"Niña! Quitese los zapatos!"

Conchita hesitated one flying second, scuffed off her calf-hide shoes, and burrowed under the blankets like a fat brown bear cub. Eduardo, newly arrived at an age of modesty, undressed in the cocina and said his prayers in private. As an after-thought he asked protection for his mother from gringo robbers, and, a little hesitatingly, success for his powder experiment. He was doubtful of the propriety of requesting aid for so trivial a thing as mud-pie powder-making but solaced himself with the thought that the Virgin had once been a little girl and besides it was only a tag end to the important requests.

His mother listened but did not smile. She said, "I hope papa finds dry wood for a fire tonight. If he doesn't get the stones hot enough the tortillas will be tough." She tucked the blankets around them and well under the rawhide springs. Eduardo noticed how soft her hands were as they trailed over his face before she kissed him and told Conchita her story. Her voice had the low husky sweetness of the native Californians. Her hair gleamed blue-black in the guttering candle flame throwing sooty wavy shadows on the irregular adobe bricks.

"Good-night hijitos."

"Mama, will the gringos come here tonight?"

"Papa will drive them away. Go to sleep."

"If they come, call me mamma."

"Yes, Eduardo."

She picked up the candle and half closed the door. Eduardo could see the smooth plumpness of her face with the queer upthrown shadows from the candle just below her chin. Her eyes seemed curiously soft and moist as she looked back. He could tell by the soft sound of her footsteps that she had moved across the room to the brazier and was standing there. The house seemed cold and empty without father's rollicking voice and his soft Irish accent to the familiar Spanish words.

The damp cold pressed down like a weight in the darkness as though the wind on the roof were standing on it and making little moaning sounds of disappointment as it whirled around the bare flat eaves. Eduardo could not see the strings of maize and pepper now but he knew they were there from the rustle, like gringo robbers stealing down on them, moving stealthily towards the bed.

CHAPTER V

IN THE morning the rain was gone. It had been unseasonably early in late September. Now the sun shone hot on the damp earth burning out the wisps of fog that clung to the edges of the hills and thickened in the canyons. They were awakened by screeching of carreta wheels on the sandy road. It was Santiago de Cerrero and his wife Inez bound for the Mission of San Gabriel. The fat oxen stopped of their own accord and the two alighted to accept hot tortillas from the Indian maid and gossip with Maria.

"Better come with us to the Mission," Santiago said. "The jail-scourings of all nations, hunted men, have gathered about this man Merrit. Now they are plundering and burning up and down the country. They are no respecters of women, los coches locos."

"Sh!" she said. "I do not want the children to hear. Don Juan is with the lanceros. I am going to stay here."

Santiago swore softly. "I think it is foolish to fight the United States."

"Si!" She nodded. "Juan thinks so. But he is simpático with his neighbors. He goes as a gesture of friendship."

Santiago shrugged and lighted a cigarette. "You will not go with us to the Mission?"

"I must be here with the rancho, waiting with the children when Juan comes back."

Inez lighted her brown cigarette from her husband's. She made softly syrupy sounds of disapproval. "It is the madness to remain," she said heavily.

Santiago glanced up at the big powder horn. "You have plenty of good gunpowder?" he asked.

Maria shook her head. "Only some Mojave powder that does not bang."

"We hope to get some at the Mission. The padres make powder from time to time. Sometimes it is good but very often it only fizzles." Santiago scowled and snapped his ox stick at a lizard peering cautiously from the wall. "Come!" he said to his wife. "It is a long journey. We must be going." He gathered grass from along the roadside and stuffed it between the wooden axles and the solid wood wheels of his carreta. Long after the slow moving oxen had disappeared among the laurels they could hear the high drawn squeal of the ungreased axles.

"They are fraidy foxes," said Conchita giggling.

"Big fat foxes." Eduardo smiled.

"You muchachos mustn't make fun. They are good neighbors."

MARIA stared down the road after the departing carreta. She wondered whether Juan would be back soon. She wondered about the hunted men who were no respecters of women and children. Everything had been so happy and peaceful until the Yankees came. Now they were everywhere and many of them were bad. She remembered the innocent Californios who had been shot in cold blood. Even Kit Carson had bragged of his hand in the affair. Women had been raped and killed. Their own little rancho was out of the way, hard to find, but it was on the road, not far from El Camino Real. She decided to watch very carefully along the road that day.

She talked to the children all through their breakfast of gruel and tortillas so that they wouldn't be frightened. To the north towards San Fernando they heard the sounds of muskets, little popping sounds a long ways off.

"Are there gringos in the hills, mama?"

"No, I don't think so. Papa and the lanceros will drive them away. There's nothing to be worried about, ninos."

Conchita teased to play in the canyon and went around pouting at her mother's stern refusal. After a time they went for a walk, Conchita puffed out in boots, leggings, and soft cow-hide jacket until she looked like a fat brown gopher waddling through the yuccas. Their mother steered them up the hillside to a promontory where they could look down on the house and corrals. Here they could see west to the ocean over the Santa Monica palisades and east as far as the Canyon de Los Laureles. South they could follow the coastline until it lost itself in the haze by San Pedro. Southeast they could just distinguish the flat tops of the houses about the plaza of the Pueblo de Los Angeles.

Eastward they could see a file of riders like tiny black ants moving down from Cahuenga pass.

"Are they Yankees, mama?"

"Hush, Conchita! I don't know."

Eduardo strained his eyes but could make out no detail of dress or accoutrements. Still he thought, if they were Californios they would be galloping. He saw his mother's tense look and knew that she was afraid. "I think we'd better go down now," she said, making her voice sound calm and natural.

It was downhill, wet and slippery.

Conchita bounded and rolled in an avalanche of loose stones shouting like a vaquero. Eduardo and his mother walked in silence. The sun was hot overhead yet a cool sea-breeze fanned their faces—true California weather.

Inside the house it was cool, almost cold. Maria said suddenly, "Siesta time!" and put the wailing conchita to bed. She came back looking pale and nervous.

CHAPTER VI

THROUGH the open door she could see Eduardo in the powder shed rolling the black grains back and forth in a skin to polish them. She wished a little hysterically that he were far away. He was too young and small to be of any help yet too old to look like a child. She had some wild instinct to sacrifice herself for the children but she was not sure exactly how. Mechanically she slipped off the bull-hide zapatos and forced her feet into the high red wooden-heeled shoes from the chest. Her feet tapped a fandango; her hips swayed.

Again she opened the great camphorwood chest, covered with mottled calfskin and studded with gold-headed nails. She lingered lovingly over the bright-hued scarfs and mantillas—las donas of her wedding day. With fingers that fumbled a little she slid out of her dress and surveyed herself in the long Boston mirror. True she was a trifle plump but the neck-line was still good and her stomach flat. She pulled out a black silk dress from Mexico and patted out the wrinkles, wriggling into it and working the silk into place about her body. The rich hand-made lace lay soft and creamy at her throat.

Conchita whimpered a bit from the other room so Maria sang gay snatches of a fandango so that she would not feel alone. Over her head she draped a shawl that shimmered in graceful folds to the floor, soft yellow background sprayed with embroidered roses of Castile, light shell pink shading to bright crimson, and a knotted fringe of heavy lace. Then she sat down on the chest and waited. She could hear the tiny trickle of water from the spring that gurgled down from the hills and drained through the rear of the tras corral. The wind seemed to be dying and the cold coming in again from the desert. She heard the high dry crack of New York powder in long hunting rifles to the east. Local smoothbores would cough with a low deep growl so she knew that these were gringos and close by. Suddenly she was glad that John was far away with his twelve-foot lance and fizzly powder. Maybe they wouldn't find El Rancho Pinacate hidden among the laurels and live oaks at the edge of the hills.

It was then that she heard the pounding of the horses and saw the tops of the heads above the bushes.

CHAPTER VII

THERE were four of them, great hairy men, riding slumped down on their horses. They looked wild and savage in worn buckskin shirts with red eyes peering out from a tangle of hair and beard. At sight of them the Indian servants, men and women, scuttled through the gate and to the laurel bushes, out of sight. Maria had not expected help from them. Her heart almost stopped beating and then began to pound heavily. The four were drinking whiskey from army canteens and

at the door. "Buenos dias, Senores."

They pulled up in the corral and sat on their horses looking at her. The leader squirted a stream of tobacco juice against the wall of the house.

The big man laughed and dealt the boy a backhand slap

their long hunting rifles made a dark cross along each saddle bow. The sign of the cross. Her mind worked stiffly wondering what it might mean.

She stood up slowly and met them

"'Nother greaser wench," he growled. "You boys round up the cattle. I'll tend to her." He threw a leg over the side of his horse and slid to the ground. "Got any liquor?"

She brought fiery aguardiente hoping that it would stupefy them. They drank direct from the jug, spurning her tray of glasses. But the brandy seemed only to toughen them; the hands on the stocks of the long rifles remained firm and steady. "Give us a kiss!" The leader leered over her, his arm about her waist. She shrank back against the door, only his arm holding her from falling.

It was then that Eduardo saw red. His Irish-Spanish nature rose hot and he charged the big bearded man with his tiny cuchillo knife thrust forward, rapier fashion, in his right hand. The big man laughed and dealt the boy a backhand slap with his open palm that spun Eduardo over backwards and left him bleeding and gasping on his side, his left shoulder plowing into the soft dirt.

The bearded one guffawed and turned again to the choking Maria. "Come on! Into the house with you, gal."

"Hold on there!" A thin hard-faced man called from his horse. "We agreed to throw dice for the wenches."

"Ain't I leader?" the big man blustered.

"Best four outa five wins." It was a growl enforced by the long rifles pointing down at the doorway.

"All right! All right! Get us some grub then."

She dared not look at Eduardo for fear of drawing attention to him. The men followed her to the bodega and brought out an armload of the dried jerky. One kindled a fire in the barbecue pit. The meat was hung on ramrods to roast. Dice were produced and the men squatted about the fire throwing the cubes against an old cowhide. Her face tingling, her breast heaving, Maria edged towards the house.

CHAPTER VIII

EDUARDO dragged himself to his feet, tears of rage and humiliation plowing down his cheeks. By an instinct of habit he staggered to the powder house and sank down on the step. There lay the powder, half on the table, half on the floor where he had spilled it in his berserk charge. He dragged the little cannon to the center of the room. Prayers formed on his lips. He scooped a handful of the black grains from the table and added nearly as much more from the floor. He poured it down the brass maw, ramming his handkerchief after as wadding.

He looked down at the barbecue pit. The men were grouped about the skin shaking dice, his mother still on the edge of the group. He felt so numb that he could hardly move. He heard the oaths and threats; his hands shook and he steadied himself against the door. There was not a piece of iron or a pebble in the room and he didn t dare to go outside. From a shelf he took down his gourd bank. About thirty small copper and silver coins rattled out in his hand and down the throat of the cannon. He rammed a sock down hard on top of the coins then dragged the cannon to the doorway and pointed it at the group around the fire.

A reata should have been around the breach of the cannon to ease the recoil, he remembered, but it was too late now. He stuffed an old serape behind it, primed the fire-hole, and crouched trembling, flint and steel in hand. A ruffian threw an arm about his mother's waist and they struggled silently, edging away from the fire. He heard a volley of oaths, saw a man stand up. "I git the gal," he heard the man shout. His mother screamed, jerked away, and started to run.

He remembered scratching the flint upon the steel, seeing the powder catch in a thin little spiral of smoke. It fizzed for an instant, smoking out of the priming hole. He gabbled a pater fast, his heart sinking with each word—another batch of fizzy powder. Then the gun roared, springing high and back, catching him in the middle as he bent over.

He awoke to Conchita sobbing in a corner and his mother bending over him. He tried to get up but his whole body seemed smashed and he had no strength. He could not take it all in and he closed his eyes wearily.

CHAPTER IX

HIS father and twenty lanceros riding hard at the sound of the shot found them so: Conchita still wailing and Maria in all her finery sitting on the floor with Eduardo's head in her lap. The men found the bodies of two of the brigands shot almost to pieces and bloody trails where two more had dragged to their horses and ridden off. Six lanceros darted in pursuit.

Don Juan swore a round Irish oath. "Who shot them?"

"Eduardo, with Father Junipero's old cannon."

"But the powder! My God, where did he get the powder?"

Eduardo's eyes opened. "I made it by my own formula, and I shot away all the money I was saving for a chemistry book."

The lanceros gathered tight about. One of them lifted the tiny cannon and swore softly at its weight. Another glanced back at the torn and bloody bodies near the fire. "Caramba!" he whispered in a hushed awed voice.

John raised the boy tenderly in his arms, all Spanish forgotten. "Begorra, I've whelped me a man as well as a chemist, by all the saints in Ireland." He set his son on his feet where he stood proud and a bit wabbly.

"Viva Eduardo!" shouted the lanceros. "Viva California! Caramba!"

Conchita stopped crying and regarded them soberly. "I'm hungry," she said.

Hand-Cutting

THE NAME of Antwerp (one of the largest and best fortified cities in Belgium) is supposed to have originated from the words handwerpen (hand-throwing). It is told that a blood-thirsty robber chief indulged in the habit of cutting off his prisoners' hands and throwing them into the river Scheldt.

Some basis for this myth possibly may be found in the fact that the coat-of-arms of Antwerp consists of two hands and a castle. The heralds and poets in the golden age of ancient chivalry are understood to have displayed scrupulous care before recognizing any claims to armorial insignia.

Hand-cutting was a gruesome but not uncommon practice in medieval Europe. It was brought over from a savage past in the custom of cutting off the right hand of a man who had died without an heir and sending it as proof of his death to the feudal lord.

—Charles S. Bentley, Jr.

Enemies of the Duke

by KENNETH BARBER

Illustrated by MAURICE ARCHBOLD, Jr.

THE Duke of Wurttemberg, Elector of the Holy Roman Empire and most powerful of its Princes, strode up and down the chamber in ungovernable rage. By the table stood Benedict, Bishop of Thuringen, the craftiest and most self-seeking churchman in medieval Germany.

"Not more bad news, I hope," said the bishop at last.

The Duke made an angry noise of exasperation. "Another dispatch from Ludwig," he said. "The messenger was ambushed, and has taken ten days over it instead of three. Ten days! An army could have marched here in half the time."

"What is the news from your son, my Lord Duke?"

"More men, Benedict, more men! Bah! he makes me sick. Always more men! A thousand of my pikemen and four hundred picked archers, he has had, to fight a common rebel and his army of ill-begotten beggars." He paced the chamber, fuming. "Fourteen hundred men, and he cannot drive them back into the Bavarian hills. There is the Duke of Brandenburg and his army on the north, and my fool of a son must ask for more men to fight his beggars." He came over to the table and crashed his fist down upon it. "Not another man shall he have, Benedict, not one. I need every man I have to fight Brandenburg in the north. They worry me like rats at the tail of a fighting lion, these filthy beggars."

His big face, with its thick features,

was red with rage and suppressed energy. "If I could only fight them myself," he cried, "if I could only fight them myself . . .!"

"YOUR Highness would be very unwise to leave the city just now," said the bishop smoothly.

"Unwise! It would be madness! That's what galls me. If I leave the city, my brother Charles will be on my throne tomorrow morning." He drew his dagger and stuck it savagely into the table, biting his lips as he twisted it round till the thin blade snapped. "That, for my brother's throat!" he cried. "If you are in power, Benedict, never make enemies, they help each other too well."

The bishop made a deprecating gesture with his lean hands. "At least, your Highness has one friend," he said.

The Duke grunted. "I wonder!" He faced the bishop suddenly. "If you are my friend, Benedict, tell me what in the name of God possesses those devils from the hills that they can fight me as they do?"

The bishop's pallid fingers toyed with the girdle at his waist, where they shone whitely against the sombre hue of his clerical costume. "Otto and his men could never have held out so long without help," he said. "If your Highness will forgive me for saying so . . ." (he looked discreetly aside) ". . . your popularity on the eastern border . . . is not . . . well . . ."

"They hate me, Benedict . . . the treacherous swine!"

"Exactly, my lord!"

"But they love their own skins. They would not risk my arrows."

The bishop's lean face broke into a cunning smile. "But if they were bought, my Lord Duke. Men have found courage quickly when they were offered gold."

"Gold! Are you mad? Where would Otto and his beggars find gold?"

"My Lord Duke has just said that he has many enemies."

"Bah! you talk like a fool, Benedict. Charles has squandered his all and more. Brandenburg has taxed his people to the hilt to march his army through half the Empire to my borders. He cannot squeeze another gulden out of them."

"The Emperor has money enough, my lord!"

"The Emperor!" The Duke wheeled round suddenly.

"Yes, my Lord Duke. The Emperor would be very glad to see his strongest vassal broken. You have been—forgive me, my lord—a little . . . unwise . . . in angering the Emperor of late."

"You are right," said the Duke slowly. "The Emperor would be very glad to see my power crumble. He has never forgiven me for helping Burgundy against him."

HE PURSED his lips thoughtfully. For a few moments he was unwontedly quiet, and then his anger and his restless energy broke out again. "By God, Benedict, I'll beat them all! Brandenburg, and my brother Charles, and Otto's rebel scum! . . . And the Emperor's gold; yes, if he drains his coffers dry to break me. I'll beat them all. I'll teach them yet who is the strongest prince in the Holy Roman Empire!"

The bishop waited patiently, his white face gleaming in the dusky half-light, while his lord raved up and down the room. He knew that the anger would abate a little soon, and that the Duke would ask his counsel. He was right. "I can beat Brandenburg," said the Duke at last, "and Charles is safe as long as I am here. But it's the rebels on the eastern border I must beat. But how?"

"Bought men will always sell themselves again for a higher price, my Lord Duke."

The Duke thumped the table triumphantly. "By God, you're right!" he cried. "Those swine on the border must be bought back again. I'll offer them half the Emperor's money again to fight for me against Otto." He paused, and said more slowly: "Money, Benedict, I must have money." He looked bluntly at the bishop. "The Church is very wealthy, Benedict."

"I am a poor man, my Lord Duke. It would be my greatest delight to help your Highness, but . . ." He shook his head sorrowfully.

"You lie, Benedict! But your Church is not rich enough to be worth robbing; the best went years ago. Then it must be the Jew."

"Exactly, your Highness. I have the Jew waiting outside. Shall I summon him?"

The Duke looked up interestedly. "You are very provident, Benedict." His thick lips curved upwards in a sneer. "No doubt the Jew was very glad to follow his nose where he smelt a profit."

The bishop shook his head. "Zachariah, the Jew, was disinclined to see your Highness; but his objections were . . . overcome!"

"Excellent, my dear bishop, excellent! As a good Christian I see you hate the Jew as much as I do myself. We shall soon persuade him though. He has good reason to hate me, as all Jews have, but he knows his profit is safe." He went to the end of the chamber and bellowed for a page, who was sent hurrying off to fetch the Jew.

ZACHARIAH came in unhurriedly. He was dressed, like the bishop, in sombre clothes. His head was covered, but crisp grey curls escaped from his brimless hat, and his wrinkled, parchment-colored face was framed in a beard of the same grey curls. His ears and nose were long and delicate, as were his fine hands. The whiteness of his face and his slow, unruffled manner contrasted with the impatient red-faced Duke, but any resemblance to the bishop was only superficial, for the bishop's pallor was unhealthy and unpleasant, while the pale face of the Jew was lined with character and strength. The quietness of Benedict was crafty and

calculated; in the Jew it was the inbred gentleness of a race softened by centuries of suffering and persecution.

He spoke quietly and simply, but not humbly. "You sent for me, my Lord."

The Duke grunted uncivilly. "I sent for you, because I want money. The Jews have all the money in this country apparently, these days."

"We are a very thrifty race, my Lord."

"A very rapacious one, you mean." The Duke ignored the bishop's glance of warning. "I want money. The same amount as last time, and the same terms. And I want it immediately."

Zachariah shook his head slowly. "I cannot lend," he said.

"Not lend?" The Duke snapped his fingers impatiently. "What do you mean? You know you will be paid, and the profit is far too great. I never knew a Jew refuse a profit before."

The bishop glanced urgently towards the Duke. Zachariah smiled very slightly. "The bishop is warning you to be more tactful, my Lord," he said evenly.

"Tact! Bah! We are here to talk business. You want more interest, of course. Well then, two per cent more."

The Jew still shook his head. "My moneys are all out on loan," he said evasively.

"You lie! Five per cent more."

"You misunderstand me, my Lord Duke," said the Jew patiently. "It is not a question of interest."

"Well then, what the devil is it?" The Duke's temper was rapidly getting beyond his control again. "I have no time to waste in talk," he shouted. "What is the trouble? Where is the difficulty? You have money enough."

Zachariah said firmly but courteously: "I have no wish to lend."

The Duke gave it up. "No wish to lend? A Jew, and no wish to lend?"

"I have no wish to lend to you, my Lord," enlightened Zachariah.

"Talk sense, man!" said the Duke irritably. "This is no time to remember past quarrels. I must have the money. My son is clamoring for more men to fight Otto and my treacherous subjects on the eastern border. Unless I can buy those men off they will be at my back while I am fighting Brandenburg in the north. I need money, I tell you!"

"You need money." The Jew spoke quietly, almost to himself. "You need money, so you come to me. Me whom you have spurned, and insulted, and dishonored. Me whom you have robbed with discriminate taxes, spat upon, whom you would kill tomorrow if you did not realize that without my wealth you would be bankrupt. You would steal my gold and my house and the very clothes I wear if you did not fear for your credit, which is worthless without my backing." He looked proudly into the eyes of the Duke. "You do not allow me to practice any business except the lending of money, and then you call me usurer. You cannot borrow a gulden from your friends unless I guarantee your credit, and yet you call me thief. You chain me in my ghetto at curfew every night, and you would chain my soul every hour of every day if Jehovah did not give me strength to break away."

The Duke grew redder in the face as his anger increased with fretful impatience. "We have no time to talk of that now," he thundered. "I want the money, Jew; and you must lend it to me."

"I lent you money once before, my Lord Duke; and you repaid my friendship with hatred and persecution. You were hard pressed and I helped you to beat off your enemies. I was foolish, and I imagined I might receive some kindness from your Highness in return." He lowered his voice almost to a whisper. "I was mistaken!"

THE bishop, who had been silent the whole time, coughed and said, smoothly: "His Highness repaid your money with generous interest."

Zachariah faced the bishop furiously. "Money! Money! Money!" he cried passionately. "Do you think we dream and pray and talk of nothing but gold? We have souls, too, my Lord Bishop, like yourself. We long to be free to live as other men do, to be respected and loved." He turned to face the Duke again, his eyes burning with quiet anger. "You were tolerant to me, my Lord Duke, because you knew you would need my help again. But I can feel for others, too; and you have trampled my people under your feet like so much dirt!" His clear eyes looked into the Duke's bravely and fearlessly. "Why should I lend money to kill the beggars who have rebelled against your cruel injustice? They have suffered, as my people have, at your hands. If I lend you money to fight them, I shall be murdering them. The law of Moses says: Thou shalt not kill!"

The Duke made a supreme effort to contain his bursting rage and impatience. "One more time, Jew, will you lend?"

Zachariah answered quietly: "No!"

"Then, by Heaven! You shall lose it all." The suppressed energy broke out uncurbed, and he spoke quickly, eagerly. "There must be gold in his house, Benedict, for all its meanness. Search it! Search every Jew's house in the city! Every gulden shall be taken. You said I dare not, Jew. Well, my enemies are clamoring at my heels and I dare do anything; except be beaten. My credit can go to the devil. My friends can shout for their money, and they will not get it. I will rule without the help of your usurers and their gold. And, by Heaven! Jew, you shall hang from the battlements of my castle."

He bellowed for pages, and stamped up and down the room, shouting orders to the bishop. "Benedict! Dispatches to Ludwig immediately that money is coming to buy off the traitors! Dispatches to my army in the north that if they break through the frontier all the loot shall be their own. And a thousand gulden on Brandenburg's head!"

His eyes rested accidentally on the broken dagger that lay on the table, half of its blade still buried in the wood, and he smiled cruelly. "Benedict, send men to take my brother and bring him here. This is a time to throw prudence to the winds. When Charles is safe in my dungeon, where the rats may eat his bones, I can go myself to put my sword through the guts of Otto and his beggars. After that, Brandenburg, if he has not already fallen. And then . . . the Emperor!"

Benedict hurried to the portal to do the Duke's commands, but he stopped suddenly and drew back in amazement. He put his hands to his eyes to ward off what he saw. There was a look of horror on his face, and his voice sank till it was almost inaudible. "Otto! . . ." he gasped.

The Duke wheeled round. He found himself facing the rebel and a score of men, all with drawn swords. His hand went to his own sword.

Otto spoke coldly and superciliously, his thin lips drawn in the bitter smile of one who had had to fight for the right to smile. "Your soldiers keep a very poor watch," he said, "or the news of your son's defeat has traveled slowly. My army is camped inside the city walls. You are my prisoner."

Rage and abuse were struggling to speak in the Duke, but he could only mutter savagely: "The Emperor's gold!"

Otto laughed. "You credit me with powerful friends," he said. "I had no money from the Emperor."

The Duke looked round the room, as if for an explanation. He found it in the quiet smile of the Jew.

"My people's chains are broken now!" said Zachariah quietly.

The Big Thicket

PINE-ROOTERS roam the secret inner trails; great scars careen high up on huge tree-trunks, left there by the vicious claws of huge black bears; the jungle teems with every form of wild life found in the south temperate zone. That, briefly, is the Big Thicket, down in "deep" East Texas.

When you think of the "wild West" you naturally think of West Texas. Yet the wildest spot in Texas, and one of the wildest in North America, is the Big Thicket in Southeast Texas. Civilization pushed in on the Big Thicket more than a hundred years ago, yet the Thicket itself remains unconquered today, one of the strangest spots on the continent.

The heart of the Big Thicket occupies most of Polk county, Texas. It extends over into half a dozen other nearby counties.

As a bird, soaring high above the earth, sees the Big Thicket, it is a vast plain of irregular but solid green, in summer and winter alike, broken here and there by a tiny rivulet, choked on both sides by dense vegetation.

To the adventurer who chances a trail leading off from the few roads that penetrate the Thicket, it is a hunter's paradise and the entomologist's heaven.

A dense growth of tall pine forms a perpetual canopy high above the damp, semi-marshy earth. Heavy undergrowth makes a tropical jungle transplanted far up in the temperate zone.

The jungle teems with wild life, the most interesting of which, from the sportsman's viewpoint, is the pine-rooter. That is a species of wild hog, possibly a cross between the "razor-back" of East Texas of fifty years ago and the vicious javalina of the Texas border country. Deer roam in large herds through the dense brush; a few bears still mark their signs on the trunks of great pines; catamounts make life uncertain for the myriads of birds that live and breed there.

The numerous somnolent streams nourish huge alligators, and turtles that are as old as man's knowledge of North America. Huge lizards lazily scale the great trees.

There are thousands of acres within the Thicket that have never been trodden by man, and far into the heart of the jungle live the Alabama Indians, there when the first white men penetrated the Thicket and still there, living a life as primitive as their ancestors lived when the Spaniards first marked a trail through Texas.

And far into the Big Thicket, too, is the "Puzzle Woods," where the amateur explorer loses himself and tramps perhaps for hours in a circle, because every tree, every mark he finds, looks exactly the same.

The Big Thicket stands still as a challenge to progress, a puzzle to all who have penetrated its depths.—Ruel McDaniel.

Crabbe at Caborca

by Edwin Hunt Hoover

THE filibustering expedition led by Henry A. Crabbe eighty-one years ago is a neglected epic of heroism. If it had been successful—as might easily have come to pass if Crabbe had not been decorated with the order of the double-cross—the United States of America would now include Sonora, Mexico, and the history of two nations would be changed in some vital aspects.

Crabbe, a state senator from California, embarked with seventy fellow-Argonauts on the "Sea Bird," at San Francisco, late in January of 1857, sailing south along the coast to San Pedro. Among this hardy crew were approximately a dozen men who were legislators, or ranked even higher in public life. At least two were physicians. The rest were professional soldiers of fortune, muleskinners, gamblers and disappointed prospectors whose luck had run out—adventurers all; valiant spirits whose courage was without a flaw. They were lured by promises of huge land grants made to Crabbe by Don Ignacio Pesquiera, governor of Sonora, who had recently seized power by fomenting revolution.

They knew there would be fighting. And they were prepared to do battle against Pesquiera's enemies. Their duty, according to verbal contract between Crabbe and Pesquiera, was to subdue enemies of the new Sonoran regime. Their reward for this service would be rich, fertile lands which would lie as a buffer state between the United States and Mexico.

Disembarking from the "Sea Bird" at San Pedro, Crabbe's company marched across California and Arizona to the Mexican border, where their leader issued a statement announcing that his was a peaceful band of colonists, traveling under authority of Governor Pesquiera. This proclamation was designed to serve the double purpose of protecting the "colonists" against attacks by Pesquiera soldiers, and notifying the governor that Crabbe was on his way to fulfill his part of the agreement.

When one guerilla thrust after another stung Crabbe's command it was assumed, at first, that the attacks were launched by anti-Pesquierans. Soon, however, the Americans learned that Pesquiera had consolidated all Sonorans under his banner by an appeal to patriotism, and a manifesto ordering: "Death to the filibusters!"

Crabbe had been warned before he entered Mexico that Pesquiera would not honor his end of the bargain. Here was proof of it. The Pesquiera proclamation read: "Let our reconciliation be made sincere by a common hatred for this cursed horde of pirates, without honor, without country—" Yet Crabbe did not turn back. Supported to the last man by his followers, he pushed on, determined to storm Pesquiera in his stronghold—at Caborca—and establish a personal dictatorship of all Sonora!

HARE-BRAINED? Suicidal? Perhaps. But Crabbe had an "ace in the hole." General John G. Cosby, famous retired Indian fighter, was to follow Crabbe's line of march with 900 trained soldiers, hand-picked freelance warriors whose stamina had been proved in numerous frontier campaigns. With these reinforcements in prospect, Crabbe advanced confidently, beating back one assault after another until he finally won through to the outskirts of Caborca. By what miracle of luck or military strategy he achieved his objective the record does not show.

Ninety men, including a fifteen-year-old boy, Charlie Evans, comprised the attacking force at Caborca. Along the route through California and Arizona, twenty recruits had been added to the original roster. All of them, apparently, survived the incredible campaign, suffering only minor injuries which were attended by physician-filibusters, Doctors Evans—no relative of Charlie's—and Oxley.

Cosby was long overdue, but the Americans decided to attack anyhow. Their morale, bolstered by fantastic success, made them super-men. They advanced confidently through a cornfield on the outskirts of town, prepared to blast out troops known to be fortified in the Caborca church. Midway, they were enfiladed by a murderous enemy crossfire. Five were killed outright Twenty were wounded.

The survivors reached cover in adobe buildings across the plaza from the fortified church. Here they endured nine days of terrific siege, interspersed by savage sorties which took heavy toll of Mexican soldiery. Then Pesquiera, despairing of conquering the indomitable *Americanos*—without sacrificing twenty men for each filibuster slain—offered safe conduct to the border if Crabbe would withdraw. A council of war among the beleaguered "colonists" resulted in fierce rejection of the proposal. Cosby would soon be there. Rescue was at hand, they believed.

That night a flaming arrow fired the building in which Crabbe and his starved, waterless band were entrenched. Rather than again have his men face the terrible *Yanquis* when they emerged, fighting, from their burning shelter, Pesquiera proposed that Crabbe lay down his arms and submit his command to a fair trial. Crabbe, knowing his portion would be death, but hoping his comrades would be spared, capitulated. Fifty-seven human scarecrows staggered from the adobe redoubt and threw down their guns. Thus ended the Crabbe filibuster.

THE "fair trial" by Pesquiera was a proclamation condemning all the Americans to death. No hearing was conducted. Eleven squads, each consisting of five men, were led to the plaza and shot down. Crabbe came last, and alone. At the final moment he was offered a reprieve if he would tell where gold and silver, looted from churches and elsewhere as reprisal to the treachery inflicted on the "colonists," was buried. He refused. Until the fatal volley was fired into his weary body, he continued to hope Cosby would arrive. One satisfaction remained to him as he faced the firing squad: he had engineered the escape of the youngster, Charlie Evans. This boy was the only survivor of the ill-fated attack on Caborca.

And where was General Cosby? Tradition has it that he never left San Francisco. Instead of raising troops, as he had promised, Cosby began living in affluence, according to James O'Meara, one-time editor of the San Francisco Examiner. The assumption is that certain rich interests with monopolies in Sonora were afraid that

(Concluded on page 125)

Dervish Gold

by DON WIMMER

Illustrated by
MAURICE ARCHBOLD, Jr.

KOSA JAMAL, the beardless, drew his flowing robes about his tall, lithe figure and gazed with brooding eyes toward Damascus, far to the West, beyond the vast silence of the treacherous, shifting sands of the Syrian desert.

At his back sprawled the age-old village of Bir Meloza, squalid, unchanging with the centuries. A great bitterness filled his young heart. His finely chiseled swarthy features were set and rigid. Deep curves of determination and decision gathered about the firm, thin lines of his mouth as he slowly, with the infinite patience of the East, inclined his head and spoke quietly to the old man squatted on the sand beside him.

"Baba," he said, "it is the will of Allah

that I go forth to the great city of Damascus, there to win the fame and fortune denied me in the lowly land of my honorable ancestors. With the coming of tomorrow's sun, I go. I have spoken, Baba."

The old man sat silent for interminable minutes. At last he spoke in low, measured words.

"It is well, my son. I knew this time must come. It is in the blood. I have saved many pieces of gold for this very occasion. It is yours to use as you see fit. I need not warn you of the dangers of the desert, for you know them well. But of the treachery of strange men you know but little. Beware of them. They will but seek your gold. The lying tongue of the Dervish, or the smooth talk of the unclean infidel are no less deadly than the sting of the asp. Go now, son, and rest. May Allah protect and guide you."

Jamal started forth the following morning with the good wishes of his family ringing in his ears. His horse was young and fresh. A goat skin of sweet water was tied to the high, curved back of the silver-spangled saddle. The barrel of a long rifle glinted in the glaring light of the sun. The precious pieces of gold were snugly packed in a small chamois bag suspended from a string about his neck.

His heart was light as the beautiful Arabian mare stretched her slender legs in long, graceful strides over the sand toward the mecca of his dreams. He hummed a haunting desert melody and dreamed of the riches that were to be his for the taking.

MANY days later the weary traveler drew rein in front of the squat, rambling inn in the village of Ruhbe. Jahid, the inn-keeper, greeted him and extended the hospitality of his kind. The cool, fragrant atmosphere of the palm trees was inviting and soothing to Jamal, and for many days he tarried, eating of the luscious fruits; listening with eager ears to the wild tales of the fierce men of the desert gathered there.

It was inevitable that during the many days of feasting and loitering Jamal should innocently bring forth his chamois bag, poke his slender fingers into its gold-burdened interior and bring forth coin with which to pay for his food and lodging. Many coveteous eyes watched the ceremony of the chamois bag; eyes that glittered with greed.

Particularly did the oily Jahid court the favor of the clean, unspoiled youth of Bir Meloza. With diabolic cunning he cleverly hid the evil in the black depths of his small bead-like eyes. He fawned upon the unsuspecting Jamal. His greedy hands itched to possess the gold in the chamois bag suspended from his neck.

At times Jahid exchanged knowing looks with Ali Mahmoud, the toothless Dervish who squatted cross-legged on the hard dirt floor by the door, his great, lusterless eyes staring blankly off into space. Seeing all, knowing all. Often these two engaged in deep consultation.

Curious glances were exchanged between the hardened Bedouins of the village as they watched the three men; the two, old, evil, unscrupulous; the other, young, inexperienced in the ways of men. But no man moved to interfere. It was the way of the desert. No true Bedouin ever questions the motives of a holy man. They full well knew the murderous nature of the *faqir*, and the meaning of the looks exchanged between the inn-keeper and the holy man.

The night of the day previous to his departure, Jamal announced he would leave the following morning for Damascus.

Jahid came forward and placed his hand upon Jamal's shoulder. His manner was suave, ingratiating.

"Allah be praised, son," he said, "I wish you a journey that will be most pleasant and profitable. Be on your guard, my friend, for evil bandits roam the waste lands beyond Ruhbe. But you may meet with the *faqir,* for he leaves also on the morrow, and then the way will not be so dreary. Even though these holy men say but little, their presence is solace in the great solitudes of the desert."

Jamal thanked the inn-keeper and walked out into the cool of the night. As he passed the old Dervish he dropped a coin in his *kashqur.*

"Harmless, these old holy men," he muttered softly, as he drew his snow white robe about him and gazed with thoughtful eyes toward Damascus.

NOON of the following day found Jamal well on his way toward the magic city of his dreams. He had left the sands and was following a winding trail that led through tortuous gullies and deep ravines and dark canyons.

As he emerged from the forbidding jaws of a particularly gloomy canyon an avalanche of boulders and jagged rocks came roaring down the sloping walls and filled the trail he had left but seconds before.

"Allah be praised! The beardless one is safe," a voice cackled close behind him. He whirled quickly about.

The withered, bent old Dervish stood looking up at him from the side of the trail. A peculiar glitter showed in his usually impassive eyes for a fleeting instant. An almost imperceptible wave of disappointment seemed to sweep over his wrinkled features. He turned his head and looked toward the top of the towering cliff. Jamal followed his gaze.

A white turbaned head showed clearly against the clear blue ceiling of the sky.

"Bandits! Allah be merciful," he gasped.

He raised his rifle to his shoulder. The head disappeared as suddenly as it came. He held the rifle at aim and scoured the ridge with piercing eyes.

"Fear not, Oh beardless one. Naught shall happen to you so long as Ali Mahmoud is with you," the Dervish mumbled softly.

Jamal lowered his rifle. He placed it across the pommel of the saddle and sat in deep thought. The momentary evil expression in the eyes of the holy man was disturbing. The face of the man on the cliff looked strangely familiar. Could there be a connection? The words of his father came to him, "But of the treachery of strange men you know but little. Beware of them." Even as Jahid had also warned him.

Jahid! That was he on the cliff! That peculiarly square-shaped head, there was none other like it in all Syria.

"But what of the old Dervish?" he pondered silently. "Surely he would not attack a traveler for his gold?"

The droning voice of the holy man broke in on his meditation.

"Allah has decreed that I go to Damascus. I shall accompany the beardless one," he said.

So saying, he set out with long strides and followed alongside the Arabian mare until the setting of the sun warned it was time to make camp. Jamal gathered wood from withered trees in nearby gullies and canyons and built a roaring fire. The old Dervish quickly prepared coffee. Long after the desert night had descended, the two oddly contrasted men sat by the fire, each concerned with his own thoughts. Presently Jamal arose. His face was impassive; his eyes avoided the Dervish.

"I go now and sleep until the moon is high in the heavens. Whereupon you shall awaken me, and I will stand watch until the coming of the sun," he said quietly.

Taking his blankets under his arm, he went beyond the edge of the circle of light cast by the camp-fire and lay down upon the sand.

Now Jamal had no intention of sleeping. The events of the day weighed heavily upon his young mind. The warning of his father rang out clear and strong, "Beware of the lying Dervish."

He had many things to do before the night progressed too far. Plans were already taking shape in his mind. He went about his tasks unhurriedly. Silently and efficiently he labored. Soon the shape of a sleeping man apparently lay stretched upon the sand, with turban peeping from underneath a protecting blanket. Satisfied at last with his handiwork, he quietly crawled farther into the gloom and crouched behind a friendly bush, waiting for the *faqir* to strike.

HOURS passed. The watching Bedouin's eyes grew heavy with sleep. The moon was fast approaching its zenith.

Suddenly the quiet figure of the Dervish arose from beside the dying fire. It cautiously approached the huddled pile of rocks and blankets beyond the circle of light. In his right hand he carried a *takouba,* its polished blade gleaming in the pale shafts of moon radiance.

Jamal stiffened, wide awake now. His finger curled about the trigger of his long rifle.

The Dervish listened intently a moment, hesitated, and went back to his place by the fire. He heaped on more wood and gazed about at the dancing shadows reaching long fingers into the gloom of the night. A sigh of relief escaped from Jamal's compressed lips. Perhaps he had been mistaken after all. Mayhap the holy man merely wanted to make sure that his companion was

"Allah be praised! The beardless one is safe," a voice cackled close behind him.

comfortable. But the blood of countless centuries of generations of oppressed ancestors, ran through his veins. The beardless one still sat immovable, the index finger of his right hand crooked about the trigger of his rifle, waiting, tense, ready.

Soon, with great caution, the Dervish arose again. He slinked stealthily toward the pile of rocks and blankets. He stood bent, silent, his gaunt figure silhouetted against the light of the fire.

His long right arm slowly raised. The blade of the *takouba* flashed, hung poised an instant, then dropped.

In that instant Jamal jerked his trigger finger.

A stab of flame. A sharp report. The Dervish pitched forward over the dummy and lay still.

Jamal never missed. Something tugged now at his heart. This was his first spilling of human blood; his first human kill. He was very young. He ran to the still form, knelt down beside it.

Presently the dying Dervish opened his great eyes, the glaze of death in them, and spoke softly.

"Oh beardless one, this night have you rendered Ali Mahmoud a great service. With the spilling of my blood, by the grace of Allah, have you cleansed me of my sins, of which there are many. The letting of my life blood has atoned for the blood of the many lives I have taken. Great shall be your reward. Praise Allah!"

The old Dervish closed his eyes. A faint rattle sounded in his withered throat. A tremor shook his gaunt body. Allah claimed another soul. Jamal gently placed the emaciated remains under some rocks. His heart was heavy. His mind was filled with foreboding. No good could come from taking the life of a holy man. The deed would bring nothing but bad luck and dire misfortune, despite the prediction of reward made by the dying *faqir*.

TRUE enough, misfortune pursued Jamal in Damascus. At the end of two years, discouraged, his small horde of gold gone, he packed his few possessions and started back across the desert waste lands toward the home of his ancestors.

An irresistible impulse led him after many days to the scene of the fatal camp.

He knew not what to expect. Many travelers and caravans had passed over the trail since that gory night. Jamal was no longer the beardless one. Two years of hardship and disappointment had left their mark. But this had been his first spilling of human blood. He remembered vividly that he had hidden the body of the old Dervish far off the beaten trail. Winds had done their share in obliterating the evidence of his deadly aim.

The gnarled stump of a withered willow jutted from the restless shifting sands. He smiled grimly. He was not far away. The peculiar formation of the jagged rocks nearby told him that he had at last arrived at the spot. For many hours he poked around. He was rewarded with the discovery of a leg bone, no doubt dislocated by the voracious vultures. Feverishly now he dug deeper. A piece of white cloth caught his attention.

He picked it up. Something metallic dropped in the sand.

It was a gold piece!

He resumed his digging. He worked frantically, desperately. An entire garment came to light. He examined it carefully, led on by an impulse he could not control, nor fathom.

The garment was lined with gold pieces! A fabulous fortune! Allah was just! Allah be praised! Here was the fortune he sought.

The prophecy of his victim had been fulfilled. The lying Dervish had spoken the truth on his deathbed.

WITH a light heart he resumed his journey. After many days he again arrived at the village of Ruhbe.

Jahid, the oily inn-keeper, once more extended the hospitality of his kind. Jamal, wise now in the ways of men, and secure in the wealth of the earth, greeted him coldly.

He warded off inquiries about the old Dervish behind the inscrutable mask of the seasoned Bedouin. The inn-keeper, wise in his knowledge of men, did not push his quest for information. The disappearance of the holy man became merely one of the innumerable mysteries of the desert wastes.

In Bir Meloza many moons later Jamal stood with folded arms before his tent. Surrounding him were many horses and camels, and beautiful women wearing finely woven black *maliehas.*

The blood of centuries of untamed, unconquered ancestors had at last come into its own.

Praise Allah! Allah is just!

New readers frequently ask if back numbers of Golden Fleece can be had. Yes, send 20c for each copy you desire—October, November, December and January—to Golden Fleece, 538 So. Clark St., Chicago, Ill.

Crabbe at Caborca

(Continued from page 119)

Crabbe's success might open up territory to competitors; and that they offered Cosby inducements to stay out of Mexico. Cosby was killed in a runaway accident one year after Crabbe's death. Not once had he spoken of the Crabbe expedition.

The American minister to Mexico—Mr. Forsyth—investigated the Crabbe massacre. He reported to the State Department that "legal murder" had been committed. His report satisfied Pesquiera, who remained in power twenty years.

AN OPEN FORUM FOR OUR READERS

Two very interesting letters from Canada start us off this month:

Although I do not presume to take place at the Round Table, nevertheless I wish to extend to you and all concerned in the edition of GOLDEN FLEECE, my heartfelt congratulations, for the GOLDEN FLEECE is a Magazine among the legion of Fiction Magazines. I am a faithful reader of the Blue Book and that for at least 10 years; in October last while getting my copy I spied in a conspicuous place on the stand the GOLDEN FLEECE. Instantly my interest was aroused by the cover painting displaying a scene of "Roman Holiday!" How I did devour that story and was it not a ringer? Please do give us some more of Talbot Mundy. That single feature was alone worth a thousand fold the price of the copy.

Another great favorite is H. Bedford-Jones in "Coasts of Chance." I just finished "She Loved Iberville" and let me say this for that feature: My early schooling has been in French Canadian schools, and we studied and read a lot of Iberville, in fact, of all characters of the early French possessions and *believe me* this day I was with him and Brown Eyes aboard the *Pelican.* Oh, what a day! Now the other features in those two copies I've just finished are worthy companions of the above mentioned features. Please hear my plea. Give us some more of the Roman style feature and keep us in sight of the "Coasts of Chance."

You have no idea of the sum of pleasure a Canadian railroader derived from those features. Believe me, a faithful reader.

P. S. Yes, the December issue is here on my desk!

Geo. Carett, Trois Riviéres, Que.

I have been a reader of GOLDEN FLEECE since its first issue and hope that its life will be long, and as interesting as it has been since its inception. Such a magazine should be in my mind as perfect as possible, and for this reason I venture the following few remarks concerning some French words used by Mr. E. Hoffmann Price in his most interesting "Wolves of Kerak."

The title *Sieur* as in *Sieur Raynald* was unknown in French at the period of the Crusades. Its meaning, of course, in English is *Sir* and at that time it was *Sire,* consequently the chief of the "Wolves of Kerak" should have been addressed as *Sire Raynald. Monsieur,* combining the possessive and the word *Sieur,* was used in French from the 17th Century only; its combining form in the Middle Ages was *Messire.* Hence the address might have been either *Sire* or *Messire Raynald. Sire* as addressed to a King, at least in English, was not known even at the time of Henry VIII and Queen Elizabeth; they were called His or Her Grace or Your Grace, from which comes the present title of the British Sovereigns, His or Her Most Gracious Majesty.

The mild curse *Pardieu* does not seem to have existed before the XVIIth Century, at least not in that form. They may have said *Par Dieu* (By God) as they often said *Par le Christ*. Lastly the title *Comte* (Count) should not be spelled with a "p". Instead of *Monsieur le Compte* as found in the story, the proper address should have been *Sire Comte* or *Messire Comte* without the *le*.

I trust that my remarks will be taken in the same spirit as I have had in writing them: that of helping GOLDEN FLEECE in being as perfectly presented as possible. I know that French professors of the great American Universities and the deans of the Romance language departments will bear me out in these observations.

Will you kindly convey to Mr. Hoffmann Price my compliments for having brought out this fine story of the last days of the Crusaders' dominion over Palestine, and accept my very best wishes for the future of GOLDEN FLEECE.

Frédéric Pelletier, Montéal, Que.

We welcome and appreciate such constructive criticism as this at all times. Inevitably, we will make slips and get caught, but a magazine like this is a liberal education to its editors as well as its readers. But please, if you catch any errors in Spanish in that delightful "Mojave Gunpowder" blame it on our sneezes and snuffles, not us.

A new Chicago reader who prefers to remain anonymous says:

Felt I should drop a few lines re your magazine, the December issue being the first one I've read.

Well, it just sorta rolls up my alley for HISTORICAL ADVENTURE, particularly this tale of the Borgias in "Golden Chains"—and when it comes to tense excitement—well, "Dead Man Alive" really was tops.

By way of diversion, "The White Rogue" offered a pleasant few minutes. Elephants fit so well into stories—and this fellow was quite the sassy critter.

Your miscellaneous department was a nice treat—I hope it's a permanent idea.

It seemed nice to spot a few familiar names—H. Bedford-Jones, whose "Portals of Illusion" were most absorbing; E. Hoffmann Price and illustrator Harold S. Delay.

The whole offered a delicious variety—from the cold Russian winter to the hardy pioneers of our country. I'll be looking for future issues.

From the University of Oklahoma Stanley Vestal writes:

I don't think you need worry about the success of GOLDEN FLEECE. It has interested a number of people here, and they all go for it. After all, you have the only thing of the kind on the market, so far as I know. And since the Peace of Munich, Americans are showing a lot more interest in history, especially their own.

I have been wanting to write for some time and express my reaction to the sight of the new-born infant wrapped up in its GOLDEN FLEECE and lying tremulously in an humble news-stand. There is no question whatever but that you have brought out something that is fine and beautiful, something that fills a long-felt want and that can be laid unashamed upon the library table . . .

But if your magazine is going to be distinctive, let's keep it distinctive. If you are going to make an opening wedge with animal stories and other types that have no place in history, you'll soon degenerate into a commonplace adventure pulp, and the Lord knows there's too many of that stripe on the market right now. There is enough dramatic material in the pages of history to fill a hundred GOLDEN FLEECE and we've got the writers who can do the trick to a gnat's heel.

Edward F. Medosch, Cincinnati, O.

Our personal feeling is that history concerns animals as much as it does man. Of course, we freely admit prejudice in their favor, but is a furry brother any less a hero—or a villain—because his relatives and friends know him by smell instead of name?

From the Crime Detection Laboratory of New Jersey, at Chatham:

Exactly the sort of magazine that appeals to men who study and collect, tinker with and use the arms carried by the characters in the stories. All it lacks is a department where the old weapons can be discussed, described and commented upon. Not just guns alone; equal attention should be given swords, longbows, crossbows, and the engines that heaved rocks (and a weird assortment of other projectiles) long before gunpowder came into use.

Roy S. Tinney.

Just under the wire as we go to press:

I'm so enthused over the new January issue of GOLDEN FLEECE that I'm writing you now when I should be hard at work. This new artist, Maurice Archbold, Jr., has done some of the finest illustrations I've ever seen in a pulp magazine. Remember we pulp readers appreciate good makeup; please continue giving it to us. Archbold's drawings fit in perfectly with the content of the magazine; keep him by all means. . . . Congratulations on the swell tales you've been handing us.

Richard Frank, Millheim, Pa.

Many more swell tales are coming, Mr. Frank. Our difficulty is crowding as many into one issue as possible, especially the splendid longer length stories in our files.

The Legend of the Borgia Venom

by ALLEN FISKE

YOU WILL FIND in Alexander Dumas' *Crimes Celebres,* a dramatic description of how the Borgias, of medieval Italy, prepared their liquid venom.

From possibly the Appennine Mountains, a bear was caught and forced to swallow a strong dose of arsenic. When the poisoning effects became evident, the bear was hung up by the hind legs, head downward. As the convulsions proceeded, from the bear's throat would come a stream of foam collected immediately on a silver plate. This arsenical fluid was then bottled in vials and hermetically sealed, thus becoming the Venom of the Borgias.

Unfortunately, less imaginative investigators have cast considerable doubt upon the effectiveness of the arsenic after exposure to the digestive processes of the bear. In other words, they don't believe it, although, true enough, there were in medieval Italy many venoms.

When Abd-el-Mumin-ben-Ali, one of the Moorish Kings of Spain, in 1164 drove from his kingdom all Jews and Christians refusing the faith of Islam, one of those who went to Egypt was the widely known Moses ben-Maimon. A skilled physician, he knew all of the sixteen venoms then used: litharge, opium, verdigris, arsenic, spurge or milk-wort, cashew nut, hemlock, henbane, stramonium or thorn-apple, hemp, mandrake, venomous fungi, plantain, black-nightshade or felon-wort, belladonna, and cantharides.

By the time Columbus was discovering America, and when the Borgias flourished in Italy, other venoms were added to the list. They were tri-sulphite of arsenic, orpiment, antimony, corrosive sublimate, aconite or wolfsbane or monkshood, and perhaps white hellebore, and black or Christmas-Rose.

During the time of the Borgias, venoms were prepared by sublimation, by distillation, and "helped" by various other ingredients. But the total result was, as in the case of Dumas' bear, an actual weakening of the venom. So much was this true that in the time of the Borgias, neither they nor anyone else knew of any venom which would kill in dosages small enough to go in a ring. The 15th Century venoms were weighed out by the drachm or by the ounce, not by the grain.

The Venom of the Borgias, furthermore, was reputed to be slow in action, afterwards disappearing without a trace. Even in these modern times we have no such venoms, and considerable doubt has been expressed whether the Borgias had any such.

Another usually forgotten fact is that the Borgias were not Italian but Spanish. And while their morals were no worse than their contemporaries', nevertheless every poisoning in Rome and every suspected poisoning was attributed to the Borgias. Nor were the Borgias accused only of envenoming.

Crimes of every shade and hue were attributed to them, and especially to Lucretia Borgia. Actually, the poet Ariosto praised her as "a second Lucrece, brighter for her virtues than the star of regal Rome." And even the historian Gregorovius, in a huge volume devoted entirely to Lucretia Borgia, proved that the sources used by Dumas and Victor Hugo were but the fabrications of her father's enemies. Among the blondes in history, Lucretia Borgia has been damned for centuries by the fictitious Venom of the Borgias.

Made in United States
Orlando, FL
21 January 2022

13875256R00079